LYON AT THE ALTAR

The Lyon's Den Connected World

Lily Harlem

Dragonblade Publishing, Inc. is an imprint of Kathryn Le Veque Novels, Inc.
P.O. Box 23
Moreno Valley, CA 92556
ceo@dragonbladepublishing.com

Produced in the United States of America

First Edition January 2023
Print Edition

ARE YOU SIGNED UP FOR DRAGONBLADE'S BLOG?

You'll get the latest news and information on exclusive giveaways, exclusive excerpts, coming releases, sales, free books, cover reveals and more.

Check out our complete list of authors, too!

No spam, no junk. That's a promise!

Sign Up Here

www.dragonbladepublishing.com

Dearest Reader;

Thank you for your support of a small press. At Dragonblade Publishing, we strive to bring you the highest quality Historical Romance from some of the best authors in the business. Without your support, there is no 'us', so we sincerely hope you adore these stories and find some new favorite authors along the way.

Happy Reading!

CEO, Dragonblade Publishing

Other Lyon's Den Books

CHAPTER ONE

THE REFINED GRANDEUR of James Webb, the Viscount De-Wold's country residence in Staffordshire took Miss Anna Toussaint's breath away.

Set beyond an expansive lake complete with an arched stone bridge and surrounded by ancient oaks, the house dominated the landscape. There were more chimneystacks than Anna could count. The same went for the steps leading from the sprawling coach and carriage park to the front entrance, which was flanked by shining marble pillars. The sash windows reflected the afternoon sun as though the house was winking, suggesting there were secretive delights and opulent treasures within.

"I can't believe this is our new home, Mama." Anna's grip tightened on her small leather suitcase. "It's incredible. So big. So regal."

"Don't get too comfortable, sweet daughter of mine," Emily Toussaint said. "It's just for a half a year until the Honorable Frank Webb is ready to step out into the world as a young businessman."

Anna had heard this all before. But as always, she was a young lady with an inquisitive mind. "And what will his business be?"

"As yet, I have no idea, I don't know the young man any better than you do. But I do know his family has made their fortune in cotton." Her mother paused. "A hefty fortune, for they have this home and a London townhouse that I've heard has gold leaf on all the clocks and ornaments, and that there is silk damask in every one of the eight bedchambers."

"How very opulent. Will this home be the same? Gilded in gold?"

"Perhaps, but not in our servant quarters. A governess might not be as lowly as scullery maid, but I am not expecting chandeliers in our room." She laughed. "But I am expecting to sleep better at night now I have secured a job and a roof over our heads."

"Father would have been proud of you, Mama."

"I hope so, Anna." She swallowed and took a deep breath. "I really hope so."

They carried on walking beneath the shade of the chestnut trees that lined the long straight driveway. A red squirrel with tufty ears skittered in front of them, then dashed up a trunk. To the right, in the distance, a herd of fallow deer grazed. The air was fresh and light, so different to the smog of Birmingham. It seemed to travel to the very base of Anna's lungs, lighting her up from the inside out.

Eventually they came to the stony carriage park, the front of the house looming before them.

"Over there," Emily said. "That must be the way to our entrance."

Anna hoped it would be a warm welcome from the other servants. She was weary after the journey, and her arm ached from carrying a case that held all of her worldly belongings—not that there were many. A few clothes, two dog-eared books, a rag doll from her childhood who'd had her eyes stitched on so many times she looked slightly unhinged, and a pressed bluebell in a wooden frame which had been a gift from her father before he'd died.

A sudden commotion behind them had Anna gasping. Horse hooves on gravel. Crashing and crunching. A loud snort and a high-pitched whinny. She clutched her hand to her chest and spun around.

Her mother wrapped her arm around Anna's waist and pulled her close, snapping the breath from her lungs.

Approaching at speed was a fine dapple gray with shining mane and plaited tail. Atop was a young man in buckled black boots, white breeches, a glossy golden shirt, and a black-tailed jacket that flew out behind him.

"Whoa there." He pulled on the reins and came to an abrupt halt, small stones scattering like hail before clattering to a rest. "Sorry about that, I didn't see you there." He was breathless, his cheeks flushed. He grinned broadly, and his eyes sparkled.

Anna failed to see how he hadn't seen them. Both wore scarlet shawls over their dresses, and her mother had on a blue bonnet. They did rather stand out on the pale gravel and with the light brown stone of the house behind.

She didn't return his smile. Her heart was thudding from fright. The horse was huge and stood snorting not more than five feet from her. It pawed the ground as if impatient to gallop once more, perhaps trampling her as it went.

The rider looked from her to her mother, then back to Anna, his smile still in place and a dimple pitting his left cheek. "And who do I have the great pleasure in meeting on this fine day?"

Her mother looked at him steadily. "I am Mrs. Emily Toussaint, recently appointed the new governess here at the De-Wold residence, and this is my daughter, Miss Anna Toussaint." She dipped her knees, a small courtesy of respect.

"Ah, I see. It is a delight to make your acquaintance." He tipped his hat. "I am Frank Webb." He paused and chuckled. "Which makes me your new student."

Anna's eyes widened. This young man hardly looked in need of a governess of any sort. He appeared ready to charge around the globe, taking on grand adventures and wild explorations.

"Ah!" he said, wagging his finger at Anna. "I know what you're thinking."

"You do, Mr Webb?"

"Yes. That I am too old to be taught anything. You presume that I must know everything there is to know about this world we live in." He flapped his hand into the air. "That I have read every book in all the great libraries."

Anna was quiet. Did anybody know everything there was to know? She didn't think so. And was it possible to read every book in all of the great libraries?

"But..." His smile dropped, and he nodded seriously. "Although Eton was fabulous for Latin and political economy, it seems I rather missed out on French."

Anna waited for him to go on.

"And your mother here comes highly recommended as a French tutor." His attention left Anna and went to her mother. "It is with great pleasure I welcome you. I must improve my French, it is the language of European diplomacy, and that is where my future lies. If I cannot speak it, I fear I will be taken advantage of in matters of business."

"We are delighted to be here and at your service." Her mother dipped her knees again.

The horse skittered to the side. He held it firm. "Steady now." He turned it in a circle, its hooves loud on the small stones. "Miss Anna, I trust French spills from your tongue like a native with a surname like Toussaint."

"No, sir, my father, who was French born, spoke English around me, for he said that was the way to find work in the country of my birth." She turned to her mother. "Mama was in France when she met him and fluent at that time already."

"Ah!" Frank held up his finger. "This is most excellent."

"It is?" her mother said, touching the heart locket that hung around her neck, something she always did when anxious.

"Yes, for I need a partner to practice my language with. So you..." his finger was directed at Anna, "will learn with me. We will be French students together. Yes. That will be most excellent."

Anna opened her mouth and then closed it again, fearing it was unbecoming. But she couldn't hide the shock from her eyes.

"But...but..." her mother said with a frown. "Anna is to be working as a seamstress. She is very accomplished, and I was told there is plenty of mending to be done."

"I'm sure there is, and any local woman can do that." He laughed. "But I need someone to practice French with, and I choose you." He aimed that last word at Anna. "I will inform my father at once, and we can begin our studies very soon." The horse took three steps to the left. "Just as soon as I have finished exercising this young stallion of mine. Gee up, Diamond."

In a sudden burst of energy, he was racing toward the long row of chestnut trees, jacket flying out behind him and head bent to the wind.

"Mama," Anna said, then gulped. The stones around them seemed to sigh with relief at the horse's departure. "I cannot learn French with the viscount's son."

"I agree. It is not at all proper." She tightened her shawl even though the sun still beat down.

Anna watched Frank Webb shrink into the distance. But the truth was there was nothing small about him. He was larger than life. Handsome and confident and with a determined yet cheeky glint in his eyes. Clearly, he was a skilled horseman, strong and healthy, too. He was indeed a fine young man if ever she'd seen one.

Her cheeks flushed at the thought of the muscular body that lay beneath his riding attire.

"Anna. Anna."

"Mmm, yes, Mama."

"Make haste. We cannot dilly dally here all day."

Anna turned and saw that her mother held open a narrow green

5

gate that sat between two topiary trees. "Yes. Of course. I do apologize."

"IT SEEMS IT is to be," Emily said upon returning to their small but neat, new quarters, "that the Honourable Frank Webb has got his way and you, Anna, my dear, are to learn French with him every day of this next six months."

"But...?" Anna set down her bluebell photograph, which she'd been looking at. "This is most untoward, don't you think?"

"I do indeed." Emily reached for her trusty wicker basket that contained her French texts, chalk, and small board.

"I am but staff for all intent and purpose." Anna shook her head.

"And do not forget that." Emily clicked her tongue on the roof of her mouth. Something she did when she was most concerned about the consequences of a decision. "But now we must hurry ourselves. First lesson is this very morning, and I have just been informed that my student is delighted to be putting Greek and Latin aside and enormously keen to get started."

"You mean...now."

"Yes, now. Of course, now. Come on Anna, do not make me late, and for heaven's sake, make sure you do try to learn your father's language after all of these years resisting my teachings."

Anna jumped up, smoothed down the pale blue dress she'd put on after a good night's sleep, and tucked her hair behind her ears so it hung in two long plaits down her back. She licked her lips, then worried at the bottom one with her teeth as she followed her mother from the room.

It wasn't that she hadn't wanted to learn French over the years.

She just hadn't seen the point. When would she ever go to France? Her father had been an *émigré* and swore he'd never return after leaving for political reasons.

"Just think about it," her mother was saying. "More and more frequently the Paris fashion magazines are making their way to England. You will be able to read them."

"I may aspire to creating beautiful dresses, Mama, but I am forever going to be hemming curtains and darning socks."

"No, no, have more ambition." She led the way from a narrow corridor with servants' doors leading off to a grand oak door. Once through it, it was clear they were in the De-Wolds' living space.

The shiny wooden floorboards held a richly decorated runner. The walls were adorned with thickly framed countryside paintings of rivers, cattle, horses, and turbulent skies, and the ceiling heavy with ornate roses and gilded rosettes.

To the right was a highly polished table, zebrawood perhaps, holding a huge blue vase stuffed full of pink peonies. The air was heady with their scent, and Anna paused to admire them.

"Come quick," Emily said. "I wish to set up the classroom before my student arrives."

"Yes, Mama."

After rounding another two corners and passing several doorways and a stained-glass window, they came to a smaller room. It was set with two chairs and tables positioned side by side. The unlit fire grate was stacked with kindling, and around it, a marble hearth with what appeared to be Greek women carved also in marble, wearing togas, holding up the mantel.

Her mother paused, coughed, then wiped her mouth on a handkerchief.

"Are you unwell?" Anna worried.

"No, no. It's just last winter's cold still bothering me. That fast walk didn't help."

"What can I do to help?"

"Open the drapes, we need light." She coughed again, then cleared her throat. "Yes, open them right back."

Anna did as she'd been asked. Her mother's lingering chest problem worried her. Perhaps when her first packet of governess wages appeared, she'd persuade her to visit a doctor.

"We have quite the view," Anna said, hands on hips as she admired the sunlight glinting off the lake. "You can see for miles."

"I am glad you approve." A deep voice suddenly boomed into the room. "It has been the view of my ancestors for many years as they learned to read and write."

Anna bobbed a courtesy as Frank Webb strode toward her.

"Oh, do not worry with such formalities in here." He flicked his hand as if flicking her politeness away. "We are both students in this room. Our lack of any kind of mastery of the French language is equal." He stood close to her and lowered his head. "Or have you duped me, and you are indeed quite skilled already?"

He was so near she could make out each of his dark eyelashes and a small sprinkle of stubble over his top lip.

"I…er…no," she said. "I am not, Mr. Webb."

"Frank, you shall call me Frank, and I will call you…" His mouth twisted as if in thought. "*Mon chou.*"

"*Mon chou?*" Anna repeated. "What does that mean?"

"The honorable young man has just called you his cabbage." Emily raised her eyebrows at Frank. "Is that what you intended?"

"No." He laughed, showing his neat white teeth. "It was not." He pointed to the right at a Renaissance picture of a cherub holding a bow and arrow. "I was going for something more along the lines of this."

"*Mon ange,*" Emily Toussaint said. "My angel."

"*Mon ange,* very good." Frank stepped back and clapped. "You see, I am learning already. You are *mon ange,* Anna."

CHAPTER TWO

ONE WEEK LATER, Anna found she was enjoying her French lessons immensely. But it wasn't the language of her father's homeland that had her enraptured…it was the future Viscount De-Wold, Frank Webb.

He'd made her laugh when he'd kept mistakenly saying he was twenty months old instead of twenty years. She'd been impressed when he'd read out a whole verse with only one mistake. And when he'd passed her a secret note which read *"tu es la plus jolie fille d'angleterre"* she'd blushed so much her mother had feared she had a fever and went to fetch her a glass of water.

"But you are," he'd said, reaching between their tables and tugging one of her plaits. *"Mon ange."*

"You have obviously not seen many girls."

"I have seen more than I can count." His eyes had sparkled. "But none with rosy cheeks, eyes the color of the deepest part of the lake, and hair that I long to see undone from its tight confines." He tugged her plait again, more gently this time.

"Here. Water." Emily bustled into the room, breaking whatever spell Frank had cast over her.

He snapped away and quickly picked up his quill.

Later, Anna had secreted the note away in her bluebell frame. She would never part with it. The tiny scrap had become one of her most precious possessions.

Right now, they were sitting in silence, copying out a list of French colors—*Rouge. Jaune. Violet. Vert. Bleu. Le noir*—over and over so they would learn them.

Suddenly a small object hit her left cheek. She swiped at it and looked up, fearing it was an insect of some description.

Her mother had her back turned and was writing on the chalkboard.

Anna turned to Frank. He was carefully dipping his quill.

She carried on with her task, wondering what it could have been.

And then it happened again. But this time, she understood what was happening. Frank had some kind of tube in his hand and a small pile of paper bullets. He'd blown one straight at her.

"Frank," she mouthed. "Stop it."

He grinned and did it again, blatantly. This time hitting her on her chin. The tiny bit of paper rolled to the floor and beneath her desk.

She glanced at her mother, who would not take kindly to her instructions not being followed.

Another and another. One sticking in her hair.

"Stop," she mouthed again. Plucking the missile from her hair and holding in a giggle.

He raised his eyebrows, and his grin deepened, showcasing his dimple—a dimple that she was sure meant he got his way more than he should.

Anna smiled back. She couldn't help it. His was infectious, and the memories of seeing it during the day filled her dreams.

"Oh, my word I have just remembered," her mother said, not turning but placing down the chalk. "I have something to discuss with Lord De-Wold before he takes off for his meetings at the factory.

While I am gone, I wish you to translate these animals and plants." She tapped her board. "We've covered them all before, so it should not be a problem. Then we will go onto their pronunciations and plurals."

With barely a glance at her two students, she headed for the door, closing it with a resounding click.

Anna burst out laughing. "You really are a terribly disobedient student, you know that."

"I have done my copy work." He gestured to his writing. "Check if you wish."

"And I was *trying* to do mine." She mock scowled at him.

"You'd finished." He stood, scraping the chair legs on the hard floor. "Now, where did my bullets disappear to?" He swept his hand over her desk, sweeping a few of them up into his palm, then he squatted down to the floor.

Anna spotted one to the right and reached to get it.

When she'd clasped the tiny weapon, she stood, only to find herself face to face with Frank. His chest barely a hairsbreadth from hers, and his penetrating gaze set firmly on her face.

"Oh!" She froze, looking up slightly. "I do beg your pardon."

They were so close, his smell wrapped around her—soap scented with clove and nutmeg and perhaps lingering leather. She breathed deep, taking him into her lungs and enjoying every second of it.

"Don't be sorry." He swallowed, the sound loud in the silent room. It was as if the earth had stopped spinning.

A flash in his eyes told her he hadn't intended being so close to her any more than she'd planned it. But now that it had happened, he didn't seem to be in a rush to step away.

She held the tiny bit of paper between them. "This is yours."

"I believe it is." He made no move to take it and continued to study her face with apparent concentration.

She was utterly still, yet her heart was pounding. She was sure he'd be able to hear it. "You don't want your paper bullet back?"

"I want something else."

The deep, sultry murmur of his voice seemed to vibrate right through her.

"You do?" Her insides twisted and turned into a tight knot. What could he be talking about?

He touched his finger and thumb to her chin and pinched it gently. "I want you, *mon ange*. You are all I can think of, it has been that way since the first moment I saw you. You haunt my dreams and fill my thoughts, even when I am galloping over the hills and should be concentrating. I…"

For the first time, she saw a sliver of self-doubt in his eyes. Was it because he wasn't sure if she felt the same? Or was it because they were breaking every rule of decorum just by standing so close in an empty room?

"Anna, you have stolen a piece of my heart in such a short time." He lowered his face to hers, swiping his tongue over his bottom lip. "We laugh together, learn together, it is you I wish to set my gaze upon when I wake each morning."

She nodded slightly for she, too, longed to look at him and no one else at the start of each day. "Forgive me if it is above my station to say this…"

"Say what? Pray speak."

"But I see you as just Frank. We have only ever been in this room together under my mother's instruction. When I look at you, I see…"

"Go on."

"A learning partner."

"Anything else?" He raised his eyebrows.

"A friend." She paused. "But we must never forget you are a young man who…" The words were stuck in her throat.

"Speak freely." Had there been a hint of hope laced with impatience in his tone?

She may as well just say it. "A young man whom society would frown upon as a match for a mere governess's daughter like me."

"There is nothing mere about you." He frowned slightly. "I have always been a man of my own mind, *mon ange*, and right now it is on my mind to kiss you. In fact, if I don't, I fear I may combust." A muscle flexed in his jaw, as though he was waiting with bated breath for her to acquiesce.

She swallowed. Her mouth was dry, and a strange giddiness had made her head swim. It wasn't unpleasant in the slightest.

Anna had never been kissed before, and right now, it was what she wanted more than anything. And the only person for the task was looking at her as though he might indeed combust right there on the spot if he didn't. "We shouldn't. I—"

"I don't care."

"Frank," she whispered.

The right side of his mouth twitched, almost a smile. "Yes?"

"But it would be a scandal if we—"

"No one will know but us." He released her chin and cupped her cheeks, held her face to his. His palms were warm and firm, his eyes searching.

Her knees weakened, the intimate, almost possessive connection utterly breath stealing.

There was a sudden noise outside the door—the click clack of footsteps growing louder.

Frank backed up, releasing her.

The lack of his body heat was a sudden loss. She hitched in a breath and pulled her lips inward, disappointment a tight fist around her heart.

He glanced at the door, then quickly sat. "Anna." He gestured to her chair.

She nodded and did the same. The very moment her behind landed, her mother strode in.

Frank had his quill poised and head stooped as if deep in concentration.

"Two more minutes," Emily said, "to finish that task. I trust you have found it within your capabilities while I have been absent."

"Most definitely within my capabilities," Frank said, shooting Anna a glance.

Her cheeks burned. Her breasts pushed up against her undergarments, and she squirmed on the seat, not quite knowing what to do with herself. Frank had awakened something in her. Unleashed a potent new drug her own body had created and now could not be controlled. It was addictive, heady, like nothing she'd known before.

TEN DAYS LATER, Anna found herself impatient for more of Frank's touch and his heartfelt words. She was greedy for the way he made her feel like the only person in his world. Lessons were all well and good, and they could swap furtive glances, and he the odd note, but her mother had not left them alone for a moment.

This desperation brought Anna shame. What kind of young lady was she to allow herself to be touched and spoken to like that in the broad light of day? To contemplate a kiss. To have her lips so close to a man's that she could practically taste him.

And what did it say of her morals that she would have walked through deserts and storms and jungles just to have that moment again?

To have more.

She was reminded of something her father had said to her before he'd died. "Find happiness where you can, *ma jolie fille.*" Perhaps those pearls of wisdom were meant for now—for this giddy, unreal moment in her life. In which case, she would grab happiness by the horns, or rather by a crisp linen shirt, and enjoy every kiss she could get.

But they could not muster time alone together. After morning lessons, there was always something she must do to help her mother or pick up mending work for the viscountess.

Frank regularly attended meetings with his father, learning the way of the business that would eventually be his. Plus, he had his new stallion to exercise. Something he spoke of often and with passion. He had high hopes for Diamond becoming a champion at Royal Ascot.

Anna had no one to confide in. Not a soul to share her joy and frustration with. The afternoons and evenings dragged like they would never end. The sun lazy in its drift westward. And her nights were full of dreams of Frank smiling, laughing, kissing her. Each morning she awoke eager for her lessons to begin. Something her mother had even commented upon. It seemed she was very pleased with Anna's enthusiasm to improve her French.

On this afternoon, Anna finished darning and stepped outside, telling her mother she needed fresh air. "I may take a walk around the kitchen garden," she said. "The heat is not abating, and there is no wind coming into the house."

"Of course, dear. Go and cool off." She looked up from the French novel she was reading. "Take your time, you have nothing more to do here today."

"Thank you."

Anna stepped outside. She breathed in the heady scent of the wisteria that tumbled over the entrance to the servants' quarters and along the brick walls surrounding the vegetable patches.

She walked alongside the vibrant purple flowers that were alive with bees, enjoying the sun on her shoulders. She wondered what Frank was doing. He hadn't gone to any meetings with his father, she knew that much. His lordship had traveled to the factory early that morning.

Likely Frank had gone for a ride. He'd taken to lapping the estate several times to build up Diamond's stamina for the racetrack. Anna had seen him from the window, head stooped and urging the beast to gallop ever faster. Tail coat flying out behind him as though he really were about to take to the sky. The sight both thrilled and frightened her. What if he fell and injured himself? The thought didn't bear entertaining.

She carried on walking, flicking at a wasp, then pausing to admire a monarch butterfly on a delicate pink rose. Soon she found herself not at the kitchen garden but heading toward the stables.

They, like everything on the De-Wold estate, were grand. A huge clock tower rose over an archway leading into the cobbled courtyard. Ten stalls sat on either side, facing each other, and along the back wall tack and hay were stored.

Standing in the shadow of the archway, she looked around. Three horses eyed her sleepily from their boxes, and a cat sunned itself on a straw bale. Atop the pitched roof, a magpie hopped, and overhead swallows swooped and dived in a constant lasso.

She walked onto the cobbles and breathed in the scents of hay and horses.

Anna wasn't sure what compelled her to the hay and tack room at the opposite end of the archway, but when she reached it, she stood blinking as her eyes adjusted to the shadows.

There was someone there. Standing just beyond a stream of light dancing with dust motes.

A man.

Tall and broad.

He was fiddling with a bridle, the jangle of the metal bit breaking the silence.

"Frank," she said when she realized who it was.

He spun, surprise on his face quickly turning to a smile. "Anna."

"I'm sorry, I came out for a walk." She gestured behind herself. "And I found myself here and—"

"I'm glad you did." He looped the tangle of leather he was holding over a hook. "I was just thinking of you."

"You were." A giddy sensation floated over her skin. "What were you thinking?"

"I was thinking." He tapped his finger against his temple. "Hang on, it's in here somewhere."

"What is?"

He grinned. "*Tu me manques quand nous sommes séparés.*"

She hitched in a breath. "You miss me when we're apart?"

"Of course. The afternoons are simply detestable. I have found myself longing for mornings."

"I, too. But they are over so soon."

"And never a moment alone, your mother is a stickler for time keeping."

"And propriety."

He stepped through the strip of light, coming closer. "There is something I'd like for you to do."

"There is?" She looked up at him.

"Yes. I'd very much like you to make Diamond's acquaintance. He was in somewhat of an energetic state when you first met him. I fear he may have frightened you."

"Yes, he did rather." She studied his lips. Soft and smooth, perfectly kissable. And a kiss was what she really wanted, but it seemed she'd have to settle for an introduction to his horse.

"Come," he said, his hand brushing hers as if he'd thought about taking it then changed his mind. "This way." He crooked his elbow.

She took it, expecting him to lead her out into the sunshine again, stealing the cover of shadows from them, but instead, he took her deeper into the stable room.

The stone floor was littered with strands of straw, and a different cat, a tabby, prowled past them as if on the hunt.

"He lives in here," Frank said. "It is the biggest stall, plus the mares excite him. One filly in particular." He grinned. "He can't seem to control himself around her."

"Oh, I see." Anna spotted Diamond's elegant gray head poking over a wooden door. "So, this is his stable. I noticed he wasn't outside, I presumed you were out riding."

"I was, and the air in here is cool for him after his exercise. I think he likes it." Frank rubbed the horse's long nose. "Say hello to Anna," he said, his features softening as he spoke. "She is my partner in French tuition."

Diamond blinked, his long lashes fluttering.

Anna could almost feel the horse and man's connection. It was a gentle tug between them, a secret way of understanding.

For a moment, she felt a twang of jealousy, then she reminded herself Diamond was but a horse.

"He's beautiful," she said. "I hope he wins you many races."

"He will." Frank stepped back and smiled. "If we care for him properly. Many laps of the estate, the finest oats and hay, and plenty of attention to his health, coat, mane, and tail." He came and stood behind her. "Your hair."

"What about my hair?" She stilled at his nearness.

"It reminds me of a horse's tail all pulled back and sat on the crown of your head like this."

She giggled, though the sound was laced with tension. "It does?"

"Yes." He took the long-plaited ponytail in his hands, his knuckles brushing the base of her neck. "I long to see it released, free, a little wild perhaps."

"You do? But why?" She stared at Diamond who chewed hay with his attention on Frank.

"Let's just say I had a dream. A vivid dream of you, *mon ange* with your hair down." He paused. "It hung over your shoulders, your breasts, and to your waist." His mouth moved closer to her ear, his breath hot. "And you were naked, your hair the only thing giving a modicum of modesty."

"Frank." Shocked, she went to turn, but he held her still with one hand firm on her shoulder.

"No. Let me do this."

"Do what?"

He didn't answer, instead he tugged the pale blue ribbon from the end of her braid and began to undo the looped strands of hair. His movements were slow and deliberate, and her scalp tugged very slightly.

She was acutely aware of his closeness, of his breathing, was that his heart she could hear or her own pulse raging in her ears?

He didn't speak as he unwound her hair like the most exquisite silk. When he was finished, he ran his fingers through the freshly washed strands as though they were a comb.

Anna was almost in a trance, quite dizzy from his attention. "Frank," she whispered.

"It is beautiful loose like this," he murmured. "You should wear it this way always."

"My mother would not allow it."

"If I were your husband, I would insist upon it." He moved his mouth to her ear again. "In the bedchamber at least, I would want my wife's hair free and swishing around her body and over mine."

"Frank!" This time she turned around fully to face him.

He released her hair, and a grin stretched his lips. "I do beg your pardon, did I say that aloud?"

"Yes!"

He chuckled and took her hands. "I have thought of you being my wife, Anna. *Ma femme.*"

"*Votre femme*? You are quite deranged Frank Webb. That could never be."

"Says who?" A line creased between his brows. "Tell me."

"Says your mother, your father, society. I told you, I am not the kind of woman to become a viscount's betrothed."

"I don't give damn about any of that." He'd spoken with feeling. "I will choose my own wife, no one will pick one for me." His voice quieted. "Forgive me, *mon ange*, I do not wish to be crass, but it is how I feel." He came closer. "How I feel about you."

Her heart was crashing up against her ribcage, her breaths hard to catch and her dress suddenly too tight. "How do you feel about me?"

"I believe actions would be better than words in this instance." He cupped her face the way he had before.

"You do?"

"I do indeed." He brought his mouth down on hers.

It was a hot, intense kiss that lit her from within, stoked the fire of her longing for him, for more of him. Much more.

Sagging against him, she gripped his shoulders for support. Her knees were so weak it was as though someone was pushing at them from behind.

"Anna. Oh, Anna." He murmured, stepping her backward until her shoulders hit the stable wall. "Kissing you is even better than I imagined it would be."

"We shouldn't be doing this. We really shouldn't...we..."

"Do you want me to stop?" He raised his eyebrows.

"No. I do not." She curled her hand around the base of his neck and brought him to her for another kiss.

Their tongues tangled, his legs pressed against hers, and like before when they were close, it was as if the rest of the world had faded away.

It wasn't just the kiss that was happening to her. It was something else. A needy tug inside her body had become like a pot threatening to boil over. Pressure was building. She could feel it in her chest, her belly, and between her legs.

He slid his fingers down her neck, over her throat, and set his palm over her right breast.

"Frank." She gasped at the connection, for it was forbidden yet so desired. She wanted his hands everywhere. Touching her, holding her against his naked flesh. Doing the things only married couples should do.

He squeezed her breast and deepened the kiss.

She groaned, sure he'd be able to feel the hard pebble of her nipple through her clothing.

And then his hand slid lower, dipping into her waist and over her hip to her thigh. He pressed up against her, the length of his body in line with hers.

She raised her leg, her dress sliding upward. He was there, helping it, his hand slipping beneath the bunched material to stroke her thin white stocking.

"Oh, Frank." Was he really doing this? Was she really letting him?

"I could not have dared to dream of you like this," he said against her lips. "In my arms, so willing and—"

He kissed her again, his fingertips on the bare flesh of her upper thigh now. A delectable tremble went over her skin, slipping between her legs and making her clench.

Bang. Bang.

Sudden voices.

"Blazes! Who the devil is that?" Frank broke the kiss and turned to look over his shoulder. He did not take his hand from her thigh.

"Frank." She pushed at him. "They're coming this way."

He didn't move but instead tensed, a wash of emotion from frustration to anger to desire crossing over his features. "It is the gamekeeper and the stable boys, I'd wager."

Releasing her, he stepped away. "I will go and order them from the stables this very moment."

"What? No. No."

"No?"

"Frank, we can't. We can't do what you want to do, you know that in your heart."

"What *I* want to do? Don't you want it, too?"

"Well…yes, but we are not married. It is not right." She shook her head. "I do not wish to be anything other than a virgin on my wedding night, even though I am not a woman of status, it is what I want, what my dear papa would have wanted for me."

He hesitated. "I do not like these rules, any of them." He gritted his teeth. "But I wish for you to have what you want, Anna, always." He turned slightly and appeared to adjust himself within his breeches. "So, I will distract our unwanted visitors in a stable, there is surely a hock to check for heat. You should slip away, for if you are here when I return, I will pick up where we left off." His face softened. "Go, I will see you at our studies tomorrow. Perhaps I will be feeling more comfortable then, for I am most uncomfortable now."

He slipped from view and into the bright light of outside, and called a greeting to the workers.

Anna clasped her loose hair, holding it in her fist. She scanned the floor, hoping to find her ribbon but did not.

Why was he uncomfortable?

Oh, but wasn't she? Her entire body felt on fire. As if real flames had licked over her skin spreading their heat. She was damp between her legs, her nipples still hard. The longing in her had only been stoked, not abated. Each touch of his tongue to hers, each inch he'd wandered his fingertips up her thigh had only made her more desperate.

Waiting for the voices to fade, she squeezed her eyes closed. If they hadn't been interrupted, she wasn't sure she'd have stopped Frank from doing what he wanted to do—doing what she also wanted to do. Did she have the willpower to resist him?

That was a question she couldn't answer.

When he kissed her, when he touched her, it was as if her mind went blank. A dreamy mist came over her thoughts, and he was all she could think of.

Frank.

Frank.

She shook her head and took a deep breath. It was time to slip from the stable courtyard, unseen and unheard.

Then tomorrow she would start another day of trying to resist Frank and his seductions. Heaven help her, she'd never last these coming months. She may as well accept her fate as a ruined woman.

CHAPTER THREE

ANNA HAD LITTLE appetite. She couldn't sleep. And she fidgeted whenever she was supposed to be sitting still darning and stitching.

"Whatever is the matter with you, child?" Emily asked.

"Nothing, Mama."

"You are quite out of sorts. I fear you are ailing."

"I am not, I assure you. It is simply the hot weather."

Emily looked at the window. The rain had been relentless for two days putting a halt to croquet on the lawn—a garden party Her ladyship had organized—yet delighting Cook, who had been bemoaning the state of the dry herb and vegetable patches.

"I'm sure this hot weather will pass," Anna said with a sigh. "And we will be served some rain to water the gardens."

Emily frowned. Clearly confused at her daughter's misperception of the current weather.

"Perhaps I will take a walk outside, when I have finished this."

"In this weather?"

"I beg your pardon?"

"Anna, it is pouring."

She looked out of the window. "Oh, so it is."

Emily shook her head. "You are fair worrying me, and you would your father, too, if he were here."

"Tell me again about how you met." Anna stopped stitching and smiled at her mother.

"I have told you many times."

"I want to hear it again."

"Why?"

"It is so romantic." She pressed her hand to her chest. If only she and Frank could have met in the manner her parents had. Both of the same class, both free to follow their hearts and not what society believed.

"Oh, very well," her mother said, then settled back in her chair, book closed on her lap. "It was in Paris, Montpellier, in August. The moon was full, the air rich with the scent of rain." She paused and glanced outside. "But the rain had stopped, and Parisians were coming out of their houses like mice appearing from their holes when the cat is otherwise engaged. Umbrellas at the ready, they strolled along the Seine, into the square of Notre Dame, and along the Champs Elysee. It was there I saw him, standing on a street corner.

"I came to a halt. Of course I did, he was the most handsome man I had ever seen. Tall, broad shoulders, his clothes weren't new but they were perfectly pressed. And he was clean shaven." She paused. Smiled. "You can imagine my surprise later when we were introduced at La Belle."

"The café?"

"*Oui, mon cher.* That is correct. And we danced, and we drank sweet wine, and we agreed to walk to the Champ de Mars together the very next day. And on that day, I told him I was returning to England, at which point, and with no hesitation, he asked me to marry him. Of course I said yes, I had never been happier than when I was with him."

"But how did you know you'd always be happy with him, Mama?"

"It was something in here, in my chest, my heart I suppose. He was not a man to raise a hand to a woman, he spoke softly, intelligently, and he put others first. He was a good, kind soul, and it is perhaps whimsical of me to say it, but our hearts beat in tune. We wanted the same things, and love was high on the list."

"That is not whimsical in the slightest, it is beautiful." Anna smiled. Her mother had just put into words the way she was feeling about Frank. And the way she believed he felt about her—if his words were truthful, which she was sure they were.

"It is a constant sadness to me that he is not here, that his life was cut short. But I know he would be very proud of you, his only daughter, even more so that you are becoming so proficient in French."

"I am enjoying my lessons very much."

Emily was quiet for a moment, then, "Is it just the content of the lessons you enjoy?"

"Whatever do you mean?"

"You and his lordship have become… friends."

Anna felt her cheeks heating. "We are studying together, nothing more." She looked down at her lap and shuffled her feet. An itch was spreading over her scalp.

"Nothing more?"

"No." She'd spoken harsher than she'd intended. "How could it be?"

"Indeed. How could it be anything more?" Emily let out a long breath, then looked at the window. "We must all fish in our own pond. That is the rule. Do not forget it. But look, the rain has stopped and the sun is peeking through the clouds. Perhaps you will be able to take your walk after all."

An hour later, Anna stepped onto the wet path that led to the kitchen garden. The wisteria had been tumbled and tossed, the flowers dripping their petals to the ground like confetti. The air smelled of grass and earth, fresh and sweetly ripe.

She took a right, away from the stables this time. Frank wouldn't be there. He'd said he was going with his father to one of the mills in town. A new shipment from a new supplier was arriving and had to be checked for quality.

It was many hours until she would see him again, and passing the afternoons and evenings when the clock ticked so slowly was getting tiresome.

The nights held little relief when she tossed and turned, frustrated, and aching with a longing that couldn't be satisfied.

"Frank," she said quietly beneath her breath as she stepped over a snail making its way from one flowerbed to another.

She went into the kitchen garden. A huge walled enclosure full of beds bursting with leeks, shallots, onions, beets, and parsnips. A hothouse along the south-facing wall housed spinach, cress, chard, endive, cress, and lettuce.

Cook's herb patch was limp after the bad weather, the parsley wilted and the dill struggling to stand back up.

But as she examined it, sunshine filled the garden. A blackbird squawked and took a low dive in front of her, and it was as if the plants exhaled with relief that the weather had turned.

Smiling, she rubbed a mint leaf between her fingers, then breathed in the tangy scent. She made for the north corner, where a gate led to the vast garden beyond and down to the lake.

The handle of the gate was a large, twisted iron ring, a little rusty where it attached to the wood. She gripped the wet metal and turned. The latch lifted instantly, the door pulling outward.

"Oh!" Had the wind caught it?

No. Someone else had pulled it open.

And that someone was the future Viscount De-Wold.

"Frank," she said, dipping slightly in courtesy. "I mean, your lord-ship."

He chuckled and nodded at her. "You know full well you are to call me Frank."

"We are not in the school room." She swallowed, her throat suddenly tight. He looked dapper in white breeches and polished riding boots, a white shirt with the sleeves rolled up, and a waistcoat of the finest silk shot through with gold. The shirt was undone several buttons, allowing her to see a hint of dark chest hair.

"That might be so." He stepped in and closed the gate. "But since we have kissed—or have you forgotten that?—we are fully acquainted."

"I have...I have not forgotten." Her heart rate had rocketed to dangerous levels. If she'd been expecting to see him that wouldn't have been the case, but to have the object of her desire, suddenly standing right before her, smiling and looking like the most handsome man on Earth, had considerably caught her off guard.

He grinned and wiped the back of his hand on his perspiring forehead. "I chose to walk from the main gate."

"Why ever did you do that when you have a perfectly good coach?"

He held out his hands. "I fear it is you who is to blame."

"How can that be so?" She pressed her hand to her throat. Her dress had a low neckline, and her skin was clammy.

His attention slipped to her chest, just for a moment. "Let's just say I have unspent energy."

"I do not understand."

He took her hand, his big palm warm. "You know I would rather be spending my time with you than visiting my father's mills. That is not to say I am not interested in what will all be mine eventually, but that is machinery and cotton and books that must all be serviced, spun, and balanced." He paused. "What I really wish to be mine, now, is flesh and blood and smells of flowers, tastes of sugar and honey." He paused, brushed his lips over hers. "You, *mon ange*."

Her cheeks flamed. Her lips tingled "Frank. I…"

"Have you thought about what would have happened had we not been disturbed in the stable?"

"Of course I have." Every minute of every day. Each dream permeated by what-ifs.

"And you are grateful for the gamekeeper and stable boys?" He raised his eyebrows waiting for her answer.

"Grateful? I don't know." She paused and frowned. "Frank we can't be together."

"I believe we can." He released her hand and curled his arms around her. Drew her close.

She sucked in a breath and rested her palms on his chest, felt the heat of his flesh through the material of his clothing. Being so close to him was like coming home—but a forbidden home. One she didn't and could never own. One she would never be mistress of.

"Tell me what you thought of when you left the stable." His mouth hovered over hers. "And you stole away back to the house, back to your bedchamber."

"I thought…I wondered why you were uncomfortable?"

"Why I was uncomfortable?" He grinned. His dimple digging deep. "You do not know?"

"No." She shook her head. It wasn't as if she had anyone to ask. "I don't."

"Then let us kiss again, and I will show you how it is for a man when he is close to a beautiful woman."

His mouth caught hers. A hungry, desperate kiss that spoke of longing and desire and a need she had yet to fully understand.

Anna kissed him back, returning his enthusiasm and energy and clinging tightly to him. The kitchen garden retreated. The humming of the bees, the call of the blackbird, and the swallow's song overhead ceased to exist for Anna. There were no rules, no sense of decorum, only their longing for each other. All that there was, was Frank.

He held her firm, his breaths coming hot and heavy on her cheek. She squeezed up against him, the press of their bodies giving her some relief from her needs but also fueling the flame of new ones.

He tasted hot and dark and delicious. Everything she couldn't have, shouldn't want, but needed so much.

A small moan caught in her throat.

The sound seemed to spur him on, and he slid his hands to her rear and palmed her buttocks over her gown.

If her heart had been going fast before, now she feared for its very survival. What they were doing was dangerous, but she couldn't help herself. Anyone could enter the garden and see them. She couldn't stop him. Didn't want to stop him.

"Anna," he murmured, breaking the kiss and staring into her eyes. "We have four more months of lessons, but I fear it will not be enough time together."

"Do not talk of our time together ending." She shook her head and touched his cheek. "But we must be careful."

"We will be. I promise" He paused. "After I've kissed you again."

This time his kiss was more confident. And it was laced with a desire that was so illicit, it felt so right. Her body responded to his, and being wrapped in his arms she felt safe and feminine.

"*Mon ange*," he murmured. He reached for her hand. "Do you still want to know why I was uncomfortable?"

She nodded. "Yes."

"It is this. Here." He drew her hand downward, over his silken waistcoat and to the waistband of his breeches.

"I am not sure what you mean."

"It is simple. Kissing you, it does this to me." His jaw tensed, and his eyes narrowed slightly. "It makes me crave you more than anything else on God's earth." As he'd spoken, he drew her hand lower still, dipping it into the front fall of his breeches.

"Frank!" She gasped. She now held his rigid cock. It was hot and thick and seemed to pulse in time with her own heartbeat.

He groaned. "Anna. Oh Anna." He closed his eyes as though her hand on him was heaven sent. "That is the extent of my need. It is almost painful. Do you understand now?"

"Yes. Yes, I do." Constrained within his breeches, she rubbed down the length of it. Eager to know its true size.

He moaned, a deep guttural sound she'd never forget. It came from somewhere primitive and deep and was thick and feral.

"What should I do?" she whispered against his cheek.

"Keep doing that." He was a little breathless, a tremble ran through his body. "Up and down."

A sudden rush of power fizzled through Anna. One she'd never experienced before. She had this big strong man, titled and privileged at her mercy. Perhaps only for a moment or two, but she'd enjoy it while she could.

"Am I doing it right?" she murmured, holding his cock firm and stroking the length of it again.

"In the name of the Lord, yes." He blew out a stuttering breath. His eye contact was unwavering. "Anna…I…think I…am in love with you and I—"

"What in the devil's name is going on here?" A shrill, perfectly enunciated voice speared through Anna's consciousness.

She turned, as did Frank.

Standing not twenty feet from them was Lady De-Wold. She had her hands on her hips, and her expression was darker than any thundercloud.

Beside her stood Cook with a handful of herbs. Her mouth, large mole above her top lip, was a perfect *o* as she stared ahead with wide eyes.

Quickly, Anna snapped her hand out of Frank's breeches.

He stepped back, straightening his waistcoat and clearing his throat.

Anna bobbed. "My lady."

"I asked you a question," Lady De-Wold snapped. "Actually no, don't answer it, I can see perfectly well with my own eyes what is going on here."

"Mother, it's not what you think." Frank raised his chin. "Miss Toussaint and I, we were just—"

"Do not tell me what to think. I saw it with my own eyes." She appeared to supress a shudder. "You were behaving in a most improper manner and…to tell the truth, quite scandalously."

Cook nodded in agreement.

Lady De-Wold pointed at Anna. "I knew I should never have agreed to let your mother bring you into my household. Trouble, that's what you are."

"I do beg your pardon." Anna dipped her knees and hung her head. "Forgive me."

"Mother, I really think—"

"Enough from you, Frank." Her voice had risen. "You have done plenty of damage already, and when I have gone to all the trouble to organize a house call tomorrow from the Burghley family and their daughter Lady Elizabeth."

"Lady Elizabeth?" Frank turned to Anna. "I knew nothing of this, I swear to you and—"

"She is exactly the sort of connected and titled young lady you should be stepping out with, with a view to marriage, Frank. This woman…" She waggled her finger at Anna, "is below your station, as you well know."

Frank frowned at his mother. "Miss Toussaint and I have become close, I wish to—"

"My wish is that you never see her again." She tilted her chin and glared at Anna. "Go and report to your mother that she is relieved of her duties immediately. I will give you until this time tomorrow to leave."

Anna thought she might be sick or faint or scream. She wasn't sure which one, so opted for begging. "Please, my lady, I meant no harm, and I apologize for the error of my ways. Frank and I—"

"There is no *Frank and I,* and you have further showed your lowly class by referring to him as such. It is clear you have forgotten your place." She made a come-hither motion to Frank. "You will accompany me, now, and I never want this mentioned again, do you hear."

Frank's jaw tightened, he made no move to go and stand by his mother.

"Frank!"

"Damn and blast," he muttered and walked up to her.

Lady De-Wold shook her finger at Cook. "And if I find out you've uttered one word about this to the rest of the staff, you, too, will be removed from employment."

"Yes, my lady, of course, my lady. I understand." Cook bent her knees slightly and dipped her head.

Lady De-Wold scowled at her. Everyone knew Cook was a terrible gossip.

"I implore you, please do not punish my mother for my mistake." Anna clasped her hands beneath her chin. "We have nowhere else to go, and I fear my mother is unwell."

"Your mother deserves to be punished for failing to raise a daughter with moral standards." Lady De-Wold sniffed, her nostrils flaring.

"Mother," Frank said, "I have to accept responsibility for this and—"

"You will do no such thing." She took his arm and roughly turned him around. "For this incident never happened, and the Toussaints were never here."

As Frank walked with his mother from the garden, Anna's eyes welled with tears. What had just happened? How could she have gone, in the blink of an eye, from feeling like she was in Heaven to burning in Hell?

And how would she tell her mother she had lost her position as governess and their home?

CHAPTER FOUR

Two years later…

FRANK WEBB, VISCOUNT De-Wold, knocked the last ball on the billiard table over the green baize toward the pocketed hole.

It missed.

"Damn it." He took a slug of brandy and grimaced at the burn.

"Hard luck, old chap." The Duke of Hillcrest picked up his mace.

"Not the only thing I've had hard luck at." Frank sat heavily in a deep burgundy wingback and crossed his legs. "I'm getting used to it."

"When are you going to stop feeling sorry for yourself?"

"How dare you. I am doing no such thing." Frank huffed. But the truth was he was gloomy. It was as if a dark cloud was following him around, a shadow stopping the sunshine hitting him and sucking the color from his world.

"I dare because I am your friend." The duke potted the final ball, and signaling their game was over, poured a fresh drink and sat opposite Frank.

The fire had faded to sparkling embers. His mother's fluffy white lap dog, Florence, lay before it, legs twitching as though running in a dream.

The mantel clock chimed; the hour was late.

"You have yet to tell me of your trip to France." The duke sipped his drink and waited for an answer. He'd wait all night. A self-confessed recluse, the duke rarely left Hillcrest. The only reason he was at Frank's London townhouse was because he'd been summoned by the Prime Minister himself on official business and had needed somewhere to rest before taking his coach home.

"France was…" Frank paused. Just the mention of France brought back a tumble of memories of his time learning the language. "Productive."

"You made some lucrative deals?"

"Yes, I did."

"So why do you seem so unhappy about it?"

"I am not."

"You dislike France? The French?"

"I have no real opinion on either."

The duke laughed. "If I didn't know you better, I'd wager a French woman broke your heart, and you've slunk back to London to lick your wounds."

"I had no interest in the Parisian women." Frank stood and stomped to the drinks trolley. He splashed in a healthy measure of spirit.

"It seems to me you have no interest in any woman."

"And I could throw that right back at you."

"You could, and you'd be right. But I haven't got a mother pressuring me to bring a wife to the estate and commence producing heirs."

"Then you are lucky. Lady De-Wold is relentless." He glanced at her sleeping dog. "In all honesty, France did me a favor. It was good to have a break from all the beautiful and elegant young ladies she parades before me."

"Beautiful and elegant, you say." The duke paused. "And that is not what you want?"

Frank sat again, an image of Anna flashing through his mind. *She* was what he'd wanted. *She* was the one he'd craved even after she'd left.

Until...

Until he'd carefully penned her a letter, one that told of his father's sudden death and that he cared not for his mother's endless stream of possible brides because his heart belonged to her. The letter had been returned to sender, unopened with—*au revoir*—written upon the pale green envelope. He'd recognized the handwriting, of course he had. Deliberate and swooping it was pretty like she was.

So, there was little point in craving her now. At least his head knew that...his heart that was another matter.

He'd visited establishments in Paris his mother would have called disreputable, but his French counterparts exclaimed where wholly necessary and labeled as *un lieu de plaisir*—a place of pleasure.

And while his physical needs had been met, the ache for it to be Anna touching him, kissing him, laying with him had never gone away.

"Your silence tells me you require more than elegance and beauty, my friend."

"Is it too much to ask?" Frank leaned forward, feeling quite earnest now he'd decided to speak about it. "To have a bride who excites you up here." He tapped his head. "One who is not just a perfect complexion and impeccable manners, but one who can laugh freely, argue a point, discuss matters that she has interest in with a keen wit."

"That is not too much to ask at all." The duke paused. "Though I am not sure if Lady De-Wold will be setting anyone before you who has a mind of her own. And even if the young lady does have one, it will have been quieted in her upbringing, she will have been trained to agree with her husband in all issues."

Frank shook his head. "This is why I am gloomy. It is not that I feel sorry for myself, it is because I see a future with a woman who does not excite me in any way."

"I understand."

"Do you?" Frank studied the man. He was tall and handsome, unbelievably rich and also an accomplished artist. How could he possibly understand? "When you can take your pick of women with no family pressure or opinion about your choice."

"This is true." The duke nodded slowly.

"So, choose one." Frank shrugged. "Get yourself a woman, a wife."

"It is not that easy?"

"And why is that? Pray tell." He took a sip of his drink, curious now, the duke had an unusual glint in his eyes.

"Let's just say, I have quite particular tastes when it comes to women."

"Go on."

"She must..." The duke paused and bit on his bottom lip. "Be willing to accommodate a side of me which is rather...peculiar."

"Peculiar? I am quite intrigued."

The duke laughed. "I am sure you are, but more details will only be divulged to the future woman in my life."

"No, you must tell me. You cannot dangle a carrot like that."

"I fear I would shock you." He drained his drink. "But that does not mean I cannot help you."

"Oh?"

"Yes, there is a club, right here in London, Whitehall to be exact, so only a stone's throw from here. The Lyon's Den."

"I have no wish to gamble on this visit to the city."

"Oh, but it is so much more than gambling." The duke held his glass forward. "Do top this up, old chap, and I'll tell all. I think you will change your mind when you hear what I have to say."

Frank stood and reached for the decanter, poured them each a measure. "So, what is the more? The more than gambling?" He handed the duke his drink.

"Mrs. Bessie Dove-Lyon, she is the more."

"Somehow I am doubting that's because she's my future bride." Frank huffed.

"Of course not." The duke grinned. "But she may well have your future bride on her books."

"On her books?"

"Yes, she has quite the reputation as a matchmaker."

"Matchmaker?"

"Are you going to keep repeating what I say?" The duke laughed.

"Sorry. Please go on."

"I will indeed. The Black Widow, as she is commonly referred to, finds grooms for brides tainted by scandal, and wives for wealthy peers in search of something other than a thoroughbred filly."

Frank laughed. "You cannot be serious."

"I am deadly serious. You know me better than most, which isn't saying much as I have few friends, and I am not one to jest."

"That is true, you do not. You are my most serious friend."

"A title I am happy to take."

"And on that note, why have you not taken a bride from Mrs. Dove-Lyon?"

"It is not for lack of trying, but as I said, I have some very specific requirements which shrinks the lake I am fishing in." He held up his drink. "But do not despair, for I have a plan for my own dilemma, which I will set in motion upon my return to Hillcrest. Perhaps, if we are lucky, we could both be wed to women who excite us before the summer is out."

"You mean if I pay a visit to this Lyon's Den?"

"That is exactly what I mean." He raised his glass. "And what is more, I shall pay the Black Widow a visit and let her know you are planning to frequent her establishment *and* what your heart desires."

THE NEXT EVENING, Frank stood on Cleveland Row before the imposing blue building that was the Lyon's Den. Behind it, the twilight sky held a single stretched pink cloud, and before it, on the cobbles, two shiny coaches and one barouche with drivers tending the horses.

Frank had been in two minds about visiting, but in the end, curiosity had got the better of him. Where could be the harm in spending one evening at the mysterious club? Perhaps Lady Luck would be kind to him in a game of lanterloo and send a perfect hand of cards his way.

As he approached the entrance, two brawny doormen eyed him from the stone steps, their mouths set in stern lines. Tall and broad, they were dressed smartly. The one on the right had a maimed hand, scarred and twisted. He didn't open the door. "Are you expected, sir?"

"Indeed, I am, Viscount De-Wold. I do believe the Duke of Hillcrest put my name on the guest list for tonight."

The doorman didn't consult a list, instead he simply nodded. He held an air of confidence despite his disability. Ex-military perhaps, or maybe even a royal guard. "The duke certainly did, and you are most welcome." Still, he did not smile. "Mrs. Dove-Lyon is holding a masked evening. All visitors are to have their faces covered at all times on the gambling floor."

Frank frowned. "Really? I was unaware of such an event."

"She believes it makes for more fun when it comes to trying to decipher an opponent's hand."

"I am sure it does."

"I see you do not have a mask, my lord, and that is not a problem. Go right in and take a right into the gentlemen's cloakroom and you will find a complimentary selection. Take your pick, but be sure to be wearing it on entrance to the gambling floor."

"Yes. Yes. Of course." Frank's inquisitiveness had been prodded further. He was good at most card games and believed it was due to his ability to read the opposition's facial expressions. He was keen to see if he'd still win the majority of his hands if everyone at the table was wearing a mask. Maybe the evening would be more interesting than he'd first thought.

The table held an assortment of Venetian style masks. All expensively decorated with jewels and feathers, some covered the entire face, some from the nose to forehead. All had slits for eyes.

His attention was immediately drawn to one that stood out because it had an air of menace about it. Perhaps it was his angsty mood. Red and glistening with two devil-style molded horns at the top. The nose was straight to the end and then hooked into a point. It definitely appealed to his fractured state of mind of late, so he picked it up and put it on.

The fit was perfect, and he straightened his cravat and set down his shoulders. The sense of anonymity a welcome change.

Who knew what the night would bring?

CHAPTER FIVE

ANNA HURRIED ALONG Cleveland Place. She was running late, again, and there was so much work to be done on the musicians' outfits. She should have been early to have had sufficient time.

"Good day to you." She smiled at Hermia and Helena, the two women who supervised the ladies' entrance at the Lyon's Den.

"And to you, Anna." Helena smiled.

"I have been advised to inform you that Mrs. Dove-Lyon would like to speak with you immediately upon your arrival today."

Anna paused. "She does?" This was most unusual.

"Yes."

"Darn it." She tutted. "Sorry, it's just I got caught up at the milliner's." She held up a hat box. "An order she asked me to collect, and now I am late for duty."

"Then I am sure she will understand."

"I hope so."

Helena opened the door. "Have a good day, Miss Anna."

"Thank you. You too."

Anna didn't linger, she weaved through high-ceilinged corridors until she found herself at Mrs. Dove-Lyon's private room. Pausing for a moment, she took a deep breath, straightened her lace shawl, and brushed the creases from her lavender dress. She hoped her cheeks weren't too flushed from her race along The Mall.

She knocked.

Nothing.

She knocked again.

"Enter."

Gingerly, Anna opened the door.

As usual, the room was doused in shadows and the air heavy with spiced perfume.

"You asked to see me."

There was a long pause and then, "Indeed, I did. Please, close the door."

Anna did as requested, then stood holding the hat box, rubbing the string nervously. She'd been keeping a low profile at the Lyon's Den for a few months. Enjoying her work and the offer of free lodgings at one of the other girl's flats, she had just enough money to get by, and she hoped it would continue.

Mrs. Dove-Lyon stood in the corner of her room, beside a bookcase, with her back to Anna. Her trademark black covered her from head to toe, her veil always in place.

Slowly she turned, her face hidden. "Tell me, Miss Toussaint, how long have you been with us now?"

"I believe six months."

"And how long since your mother passed?"

Anna's throat tightened. It was still hard to think of her mother's last weeks. She'd been racked with a bloody cough, her poor body reduced to skin hanging from bones, her cheeks almost knifing through the flesh of her face. "That would also be six months."

"And it is still hard for you." It wasn't said as a question.

"I believe it will always be."

"It is the way of love." Mrs. Dove-Lyon sat and picked up a quill.

But she didn't dip it in ink, she simply twiddled it between her fingers. "And you will recall that because your mother loved you, she set me a task."

Anna swallowed. "I am aware."

"One that I must complete as I have been paid for it."

Anna was silent.

"It would be very bad for my reputation, don't you think, if I do not deliver a mother's dying wish."

"I do not wish to do anything to harm your reputation." Anna dipped her head. "I assure you of that."

"Yet the governess tells me you have nothing nice to say about any of the gentlemen frequenting this establishment."

Anna's cheeks heated, and she shifted from one foot to the other. "I am sure that is not quite what I have said."

"I know what you have said." Mrs. Dove-Lyon wafted the feathered quill in Anna's direction. "I hear and see everything that goes on in the Lyon's Den. It is mine."

"Of course. Forgive me."

She sighed. "Anna, you are a woman with a smeared reputation. A woman tarred with a scandal."

Anna hung her head in shame. But although she may have looked regretful and demure, within her core a hot rage burned—rage at Viscount De-Wold, who'd seduced her, duped her, and then left her to take the heat.

If she ever saw him again, she'd give him a piece of her mind. She'd slap that smug smile, including his dimple, right off of his face. He was a cad. A liar. A man who thought only of himself.

"And I understand the viscount's cook did you no favors with her loose tongue and vivid imagination that choose to embellish all that was seen on that day, but that is all history now. What's done is done, and you must face the consequences of your poor actions and—"

"Poor actions!" Anna's mouth fell open. How could the Black

Widow talk of such things as though she, Anna, was the only woman under the very roof that covered them who had made bad choices. She knew the things that went on here. The top floor rooms that welcomed rich men late at night only to have them leave with empty pockets and satisfied smiles come morning. The gambling that wasn't always as fair and square as it should be. The excessive consumption of drink that had patrons betting on the most ridiculous of things.

"I am not judging you, or any of my girls or clients," Mrs. Dove-Lyon went on. "I am simply saying it as it is. As your mother told me."

"I hate that I did that to her." A familiar lump caught in her throat. "It pains me every day."

Mrs. Dove-Lyon wafted the quill again. "In the past, dear girl, all in the past. By talking of the past, we must now move you into the future."

"I don't understand."

"Please open the hat box."

"The hat box?"

"Isn't that what you are holding?"

"Er, yes, of course. I beg your pardon." She set the box on the floor and wriggled off the lid. Within it, a white hat sat on a profusion of snow-white tulle.

"Take it out."

Carefully, Anna retrieved the hat. The tulle was thick, like a veil, and the silky hat reminded her of gentleman's top hat. "It is most unusual."

"Indeed, it is, and it has been created especially for a most unusual evening." She paused. "Try it on."

"Me?"

"Yes, Anna, you." There's was a hint of impatience in the Black Widow's voice.

Quickly, Anna placed the hat on her head. It fit perfectly. The heavy tulle fell over her face, blurring her vision as though she were standing in dense fog.

"Ah, yes, very good." Mrs. Dove-Lyon nodded. "That should be sufficient. Yes. Indeed."

"Sufficient for what?" Anna asked. She fiddled with her mother's heart locket, which now sat around her neck.

"Sufficient for me to fulfill my promise to your mother."

"I don't understand."

"Tonight, Miss Toussaint." Mrs. Dove-Lyon set down the quill and stood. "I have decided to hold a masked event." She paused as though letting her words settle in Anna's brain. "All gentlemen entering the gambling floor will have their identities concealed beneath a mask. I believe this will add to the thrill of the chase when it comes to them planning their next move, be it whist or loo or piquet."

"That sounds…interesting." But what did it have to do with her?

"And as you can see, or rather can't see, your identity is also concealed."

"I am sure it is." Her stomach tightened and did a strange little flip. What was the Black Widow planning?

"Tonight, you, Anna, will stand on the ladies viewing balcony with your face as concealed as every gentleman in the room."

"Yes, of course." She nodded. That sounded easy enough.

"And when the last hand is played and a winner announced, I will have found your match. The one your mother paid me to find. Your husband."

"But…but…no." Her mouth dried. "I mean, my mother did not want it to be left to chance, the turn of a card and—"

"Be quiet, child. You have left me no choice. Since no man has elicited even one murmur of admiration in all the time you have been here, I have to take matters into my own hand."

"But this isn't your hand, this is the hand of fate. A mere deck of cards that will determine my future. What if he is a fat, rude, smelly—"

"I would not let such a fellow into the Lyon's Den." She pointed at

Anna. "Trust the process and be thankful that the late Viscount De-Wold saw fit to pay your mother a severance which has allowed you to fall under my services." She tilted her chin. "He was a good man."

"Indeed, he was." Though she couldn't say the same for his wife whose withering final look still gave Anna the shivers. She'd almost seen the hate coming off her in waves through the air. Sharp and rancid, it had stuck to Anna like a bad smell as well as driving spears into her dreams.

"You cannot stay here darning and fixing up the musicians' outfits forever. That was not the deal I struck with Mrs. Toussaint. You, Anna, must marry and put the misdemeanor in your past. Well and truly in your past."

A sudden image of Frank jumped into her mind. He'd elicited so many emotions in her, stoked her desires, and fueled a love that had made her feel as though she might burst if she wasn't in his presence. Was she really ready to commit all that to a memory? Her distant past?

Yes. Too damn right she was. He was a wretch, and she hoped he was miserable in whatever he was doing. Unsuccessful too. She hoped bad luck followed him around tainting his days and blackening his dreams.

"Anna!"

"I beg your pardon, Mrs. Dove-Lyon."

"Take your leave. I have books to balance." She sat again. "I will see you tonight at the stroke of midnight on the balcony. You will be the grand prize, and I'm sure the competition will be stiff."

Anna grabbed the hat box and slipped from the office. Once outside, she placed the hat with its froth of tulle away.

"Oh, what have I done?" She shook her head. If only she'd accepted Mister Edward Jones's offer of a walk by the river the week before. He wasn't handsome, not the way Frank had been, but his teeth were straight and his moustache always neatly trimmed. Or even Mister Charles Goldsmith of Walsden—no oil painting but always kind and polite, and he wore good cologne. But no, she'd seen not an ounce of sense, believing that she could live on as she was for as long as she wanted to.

Now her mind had been made up for her. Or at least it would be tonight, at midnight.

She swallowed the bitter taste of anxiety past a lump of anticipation that had lodged in her throat.

Picking up the box, she rushed to the ladies' parlor. God only knew what type of man would be her fate. Rotund. Ill-mannered. Slothish. Smelly. Warty. Puce-cheeked. Rank-breathed. Bad-tempered. Unkind.

Unkind would be the worst, surely. But what about a combination of all of those things. Life would be unbearable.

To hell with it. She'd have to run. Slink past Helena and Hermia and try and make a living for herself elsewhere in London. Find a way to survive on the streets until she could scrape money together for a room somewhere.

She reached the parlor and rushed in. It was empty. For that she was thankful. She needed a moment with her thoughts. They were tumbling through her mind, rocks down a mountain creating a confusing dust. But as the dust cleared and she sat staring at the hat box, clarity returned.

What choice did she have?

Her mother had provided for her in the best way she knew how. And that was to pay the Black Widow to find her a husband of means to take care of her—a husband who could withstand a scandal in her past.

There was no other establishment on God's earth like the Lyon's Den. If she walked out, her chance would be lost. Not only that, it would certainly mean her mother's deathbed request would not be granted.

"I can't do that." She pressed the heels of her hands to her eyes. She had brought enough shame upon her mother, to not carry out her last wish would be unforgivable.

Dropping her hands to her sides, she sucked in a deep breath. "Be strong, Anna." Tilting her chin, she stared at a portrait of a young woman with a pearl necklace. Everything about her screamed confidence, resilience, stoicism. Anna let the image sear into her mind.

She'd be that woman. Whatever the world threw at her or the hands the cards dealt, she'd be up for the challenge. She'd stick by her word to her dear, departed mother.

How bad could he be?

CHAPTER SIX

FRANK ACCEPTED ANOTHER glass of exceptionally fine claret and adjusted his mask. The damn thing was hot, his forehead perspiring, but the rules were strict. No mask. No gambling.

And he was in the mood for gambling. With each drink, his stakes got higher, he grew more daring, and it was paying off—he was on a winning streak.

Now he sat at the center table. His blood running thick with excitement. The hour was getting late, but he didn't care. All he thought about was the end of the game, his tactics, and second-guessing his opponents' hands. Winning was a drug like no other.

"Yes!" He banged his fist on the table triumphantly as he won yet another hand.

The dealer pushed several shillings his way, adding to his pile. Not that it was about the money; it was about being the best.

"Another game?" the dealer asked.

"Of course." Frank took a mouthful of drink and cast his glance around the table. Four other men sat there, each masked—two maned lions, a Venetian, and a bird complete with tall blue feathers and bejewelled beak. "Chaps?"

They all nodded.

But then as the dealer shuffled, a figure approached. Average height and dressed in a black gown and shawl, he guessed it was the infamous Black Widow.

The dealer nodded at her, and she did the same back and came to a halt between Frank and the bird. "Gentlemen, I trust you are being well looked after."

"Indeed, we are." Frank grinned, not that she would be able to see his smile beneath his mask. "Just setting up for another game, though I don't fancy my opponents' chances at winning any of their stakes back." He gestured to his pile of coins.

"Ah, this is not a game for money," she said, tapping her fingers together.

"So, what is the prize?" one of the lions asked.

"Indeed, pray tell," the other lion added.

Frank couldn't see her face as she wore a black veil. But he sensed an expression of anticipation, of drawing out the moment. Enjoying her position of authority.

"Perhaps it is not worth winning," he said, sitting back in his chair and folding his arms. "And if it is not worth winning, it is not worth playing."

"Oh, I can assure you it is." She nodded slowly. "The only question is, are you willing to receive the prize without question?" She looked around the group of five men.

The rest of the hall had quieted. Other games had ceased. The Black Widow held the room in the palm of her hand.

"If it is not a prize of money, it must surely be a prize of land," the bird said, his Scottish accent deep.

"Not land, no." She paused. "But surely you can guess, after all, what does a gentleman prize more than both land and money."

"Naught." The bird laughed.

Frank's mind whirred. His conversation with the duke came back to him. "A woman," he said quietly.

"I beg your pardon?" The Black Widow leaned closer to him.

"A woman," he said.

"You are almost right." She waggled her finger at him.

He hesitated then, "A wife."

"Excellent." She clapped her hands. "A beautiful wife who will keep a man warm at night, willing, desirable, intelligent, and loyal, that is the grandest prize of all."

"One that cannot be found in a gaming hall," Frank said.

"That…" still her finger wagged his way, "is where you are wrong, whoever you are, because this is not any gaming hall, and that is the very reason you are here, all of you. Because this is no ordinary establishment."

There were a few whoops and cheers around the room, several glasses raised.

"You expect the winner of the next game to marry a woman he has never seen," the first lion asked.

"Oh no, that would be ridiculous." The Black Widow shook her head. "Of course you can see her first. All that I ask is that if you agree to be dealt a hand in this next game and win, you agree to marry her at noon tomorrow without question or forever live with the reputation of not playing fair and square. A man not worth his word." She let her words sink in for a moment. "If you are not in the game, stand up now and walk away."

Frank looked around the table. Each man stayed seated. Shoulders back, chins up.

Still the dealer shuffled.

Well, he was damned if he'd be the one to bow out. He was made of tougher stuff than that. And besides, finding a wife on his own wasn't working out well, and his mother's offerings were even less appealing.

But how she would rage if he married this way.

A wry smile tugged his lips. Perhaps it would serve her right for sending away the only woman he'd ever felt anything for, ever wanted to wear his ring. "I'm in." He slapped his hand, palm down on the green felt covering the table. "A willing woman in my bed is an exceptional prize indeed."

"Good." The Black Widow looked around the table.

One by one the other four men agreed to be in the game.

"So where is she?" Frank asked. "You said we could see her first."

"Ah, but she is in full view." The Black Widow raised her hand. "Right there, on the balcony, quite the vision, don't you think."

Frank followed her line of sight.

On a balustrade balcony he hadn't noticed before stood a woman all in white. But that was as much as he could say about her. For her clothes gave not a hint of her curves, if any, and a man's top hat, white, held a thick cloud of frothy material that covered her face.

"She could be covered in warts with a hook nose." The second lion held out his hands. "A hundred years and a day old."

"Yeah, a right old crony." The bird huffed.

"I can assure you," She stepped up to him, brought her veiled face close. "I do not have any old cronies in my establishment. The woman you see up there is beautiful, intelligent, talented, and in need of a husband as much as I suspect all of you men are in need of a wife."

The bird didn't reply.

"The Lyon's Den has come highly recommended," Frank said, indicating to the dealer to start dishing out five cards to each player. "And I, for one, trust in your choice of bride for us, Mrs. Dove-Lyon."

ANNA STOOD ON the balcony looking down at the busy gaming floor through the fog of her veil. It was a familiar sight to her, except tonight, there was one difference—all the men wore masks. They were of varying degrees of elaborateness and ranged from animals to mythical creatures, and some were just a mass of jewels and feathers with eye and mouth holes. What they all had in common was it was impossible to make out any of the men's features. The only thing she could say with confidence was if they were tall or short, fat or thin.

Mrs. Dove-Lyon had swept into the hall just before midnight, her black dress billowing and her chin lifted as if she fancied herself a queen and was surveying her kingdom.

She'd come to a halt at the main table, commanding the attention of the men seated there and the rest of the hall.

Yet now all attention was on her, Anna. Five masked faces stared up at her. And she knew what they were thinking. If they were to win her, would she be a good prize?

A knot of anxiety wound in her stomach. The urge to run was still strong. Luckily, the urge to do right by her mother was stronger.

She clenched her hands, her fingernails biting into her perspiring palms. Her breaths were coming fast, and her heart thudded.

The dealer handed out the cards, and when each man lifted his hand, he turned his attention from her.

She gripped the balcony edge and peered closer, wishing she could see each set of cards and get a clue as to who would win her.

Who would be her husband?

"Mother, I hope you knew what you were doing," she muttered.

The game began, the rest of the room watched on, bated breath. The suspense tangible.

A hush, like a winter cloak, descended as cards were studied, discarded or kept, new ones picked up.

One player, his scarlet mask a hideous devil's face with horns and hooked nose, had the biggest pile of winnings before him. He obviously played a good game and knew what he was doing. But anyone with a modicum of sense knew lanterloo was also a game of luck—the god of cards getting the final word.

A few masked men moved closer, keen to see what was going on. No one spoke. The dealer stood quietly, checking for cheating. Mrs. Dove-Lyon held her hands clasped before her, her own wedding ring glinting in the low lighting.

After twenty long minutes, the game was drawing to an end. Anna had no idea who was winning, she couldn't see that far, and if she could have, her veil hindered her vision.

The devil glanced up at her, seeming to peer through her veil, through her clothes, as if wanting to know her inside and out.

It was then she sensed it, like an arrow had been fired into her chest; she knew he had a winning hand. It was the way he sat, the way he studied her, the way he held the cards to his white shirt.

She swallowed. It was as if a tight lump of cotton had lodged in her throat. Her fate was sealed.

Unless…unless he chose to purposely wreck his hand, put down a trump card, and got back into the game.

But the men who frequented the Lyon's Den weren't losers, and she knew that in the core of her soul. They played to win whether it was business, life, or cards. She'd met enough of them in the last few months to know that.

And as that knowledge settled in her brain, the devil lay down a Pam-flush, making him a clear winner of the trick.

There was a collective intake of breath from the room, and several loud exhalations around the table.

Anna wasn't breathing at all. It was as if the air had become trapped in her lungs.

"It seems," the Black Widow said, "we have a winner. Congratulations, sir." She squeezed his shoulder. "I am sure you will not be disappointed with your prize."

He said nothing, instead he just stared up at Anna. All she could see were his eyes, and they were unblinking.

His obvious interest in her was unnerving, as was the fact she sensed he was strong-willed and competitive. All she could hope for was he'd be of a kindly temperament.

"She should remove her veil," the lion said. "So our friend can set eyes on his betrothed." He chuckled. "See her warts and all."

"And indeed, he will set his eyes on her," the Black Widow said. "Tomorrow, at the altar, after vows have been made, that way, we can have no backing out of the deal. No disappointment for either party." She flicked her hand at Anna. "Go my dear and rest well on your last night as a single maiden, for tomorrow, you will have this fine devil in your bed." She laughed, a high-pitched cackle, and it was the last thing Anna heard as she left the balcony.

CHAPTER SEVEN

"HOW DO YOU feel, Miss Anna?" Hermia asked.

"Like I am about to make a deal with the devil." Anna took a sip of water.

"I'm sure beneath that mask you will find a dashing fellow." Helena shrugged as though she wasn't convinced of her own words.

Anna huffed and set her glass of water aside. It was ten minutes to noon. The ceremony had crept up on her over the morning, the clock on the mantel of the ladies' parlor ticking away and not caring that with each passing second her freedom was coming closer to its end.

"I heard Theseus and Egeus talking to Titan, they were on the door when he came in."

"Oh?" Anna perked up. "What did they say?"

If he's a monster, I'm taking my chances on the streets and getting out of here...now.

Helena screwed up her face. "It was hard to make out the conversation, but I caught the words successful and rich."

"Isn't that every man who frequents the Lyon's Den?" Anna frowned.

"I guess." She paused. "Though at least they didn't say he was grotesque."

"For that, I suppose, I should be grateful. But why would he choose such a hideous mask?"

"Men are strange creatures," Hermia said, reaching for Anna's veiled hat. "It is why I have chosen to remain a single maiden."

"You say that," Helena said, "but when the right man comes along, one who makes your heart flutter and your knees turn weak, you'll be rushing up that aisle faster than the hounds of hell."

Hell. That felt exactly where Anna was going. She raised her eyes heavenward. "Please let him be kind, not a drunk, and with no appetite for bedchamber activities."

Hermia burst out laughing. "Oh dear, you really do have low expectations."

"Wouldn't you?"

Hermia placed the hat on Anna's head, setting it secure, then fluffing the veil to cover her face. "I would have faith in Mrs. Dove-Lyon. She has been doing this for many years."

"But how can she possibly know who she has married me off to?"

"She works in mysterious ways, unusual ways," Helena said, squeezing Anna's hand. "There won't have been a man at that table she wouldn't have seen you wed to."

"You really think so?"

"Yes, I do."

Anna was quiet. It seemed her fate had been a combination of the draw of the cards and the Black Widow's meddling.

The clock chimed.

She drew in a breath, her stomach tensing, then somersaulting.

"This is it." Helena opened the door. "They'll all be waiting in the ladies' dining room for you."

It wasn't to be the church wedding Anna had always hoped for, but that didn't matter. It was hardly the groom she'd always hoped for either.

She walked toward the dining room, her bridal satin slippers silent on the wooden floor. The scent of petals and powder filled her nose. When she reached the elegant room she paused, peered through her veil, and saw the clergyman, Mrs. Dove-Lyon, and her intended, still wearing his devil mask.

If her stomach had been turning over before, now it did so complete with a swarm of butterflies. She steeled herself, hoping she wouldn't faint with nerves, or worse still, vomit.

The man she was to marry had his attention solely on her once again. His dark cut-away jacket had been left open to display a richly embroidered red waistcoat topped with a white cravat and linen shirt. His black knee-high breeches were tight, his black stockings and shoes appeared brand new. If it hadn't been for the fiendish mask, he could almost have been described as a fine specimen of a man.

"Ah, here she is. Your beautiful bride." Mrs. Dove-Lyon clasped her hands together. "Come in, my dear, don't be shy."

Anna didn't answer, she couldn't, her mouth was too dry. But she did step up to the clergyman, Hermia and Helena—who were to be witnesses to the marriage—close behind.

A clerk Anna hadn't noticed before, stepped forward and handed the clergyman the Common Book of Prayer.

"Ah, thank you," he said, opening it. "Let us begin."

"Make it snappy." Mrs. Dove-Lyon clicked her fingers, her excitement obvious. "And clerk, get the register ready for signing. The special license is prepared, you'll see that for yourself. No bans required."

The clergyman cleared his throat. "I trust there is no lawful impediment preventing either of you from marrying?"

The devil shook his head.

"No," Anna managed, her voice as quiet as a church mouse.

"He doesn't have a ring, it's at his family home," Mrs. Dove-Lyon said. "So, skip that part." She swirled her finger at the prayer book as if hurrying the words out into the open.

The clergy spoke for a few minutes and then, "In the eyes of God, and in the presence of witnesses, I now pronounce you man and wife."

"Excellent." Mrs. Dove-Lyon clapped. "That is my duty done. Now sign the register, and you may see each other for the first time. Gaze upon the face you will be spending the rest of your life with."

"This really is one of the most unorthodox ceremonies I've ever—"

"Oh hush, Benjamin," Mrs. Dove-Lyon snapped at the clergyman. "With all due respect, my donation has more than covered any 'unusualness.' And I'm sure you'll see with time, this is a most satisfactory union."

The clergyman didn't seem convinced, and as Anna signed the register, her hand guided by the clerk because of the veil impeding her vision, she sensed the anticipation in the room growing. The air was crackling with it. A fizz of tension that bounced off the walls. It seemed to fill her body.

"And you can rest assured," Mrs. Dove-Lyon said, "That I will personally make an announcement in the papers, for a lady may as well be single if the wedding is not told to all in print."

The devil placed down the pen, then reached for his mask.

"Yes, the moment has arrived," Mrs. Dove-Lyon said. "Please, hand me your veiled hat." She held out her hand to Anna.

Trembling, Anna reached for her hat. Her fumbling fingers seemed to catch in the excessive material, but eventually, she pulled it up and off. It was immediately taken from her.

And as it was, she watched her groom's mask come away from his face.

His face!

A familiar, handsome face.

She gasped and clasped her hand to her mouth. What in God's name was going on? Was this some kind of joke? Some kind of trick? An illusion.

"Anna!"

His eyes narrowed. He stepped forward, his mouth slack, as if he, too, was hardly believing what he was seeing.

"Frank!" His name scratched over her tongue. It was one she hadn't allowed herself to utter for years. Not that his face hadn't loomed in her dreams. It had.

His scent still infiltrated her nose whenever she was around horses or past by a wisteria. But speak his name? No, her mother had forbidden it to be mentioned again, and Anna was quite happy to go along with that.

"What kind of sleight of hand produced this?" Frank pointed at Anna, then turned to Mrs. Dove-Lyon. "Tell me now, I demand it."

"There was no deception, you were there, my lord." Mrs. Dove-Lyon tilted her chin. "And there were many witnesses, including the dealer, who is one of the most respected for miles around." She paused. "I take it you know one another."

Hermia giggled.

Helena nudged her, though her eyes were also wide with amusement and a smile was tugging at her lips.

"Know him!" Anna said, finding her tongue. "This man is the very reason for my poor mother's demise and the cause of me being here in the first place."

"Ah, I see." Mrs. Dove-Lyon nodded and steepled her fingers together beneath her chin, pressing the material of her black veil. "So, you could say you have a rather colorful past, the two of you."

"Colorful," Anna said. "He turned my life to darkness. There is no color with him in it."

"Anna." Frank frowned and took a step toward her.

"Stay away from me." She batted her hand in his direction. "This marriage simply can't be. I'd rather live on the streets." She turned to the clerk. "Remove my name from the register, this instant."

"I'm afraid that can't be done, ma'am, the witnesses have signed, as have I."

"But no one else needs to know, please, tear out the page." She knew she was begging but didn't care. "I simply can't be married to this awful man. He has no loyalty and lies spill from his lips every time he opens his mouth."

"You are married." The clergyman snapped the prayer book closed. "Of that I can assure you."

"You have betrothed me to the devil, surely you can see that, he even looked like him." Frustration was tearing at her.

Why couldn't they see what a hideous mistake this was. That she hated Frank Webb and had done ever since he'd walked away from her in the kitchen garden of his estate and allowed his family to banish her. It had been a weak and spineless act. Oh, she hadn't expected him to wed her then, even though she'd dreamed of it once, but he could have spoken up for her, saved her mother's job even if she had left. Because it was the damp home they'd gone to live in, with no other options, that had ailed her mother so quickly.

"I AM NOT the devil." Frank tossed the scarlet horned mask to the corner of the room where it collided with an urn of pale pink flowers. "As you well know."

"I know that actions speak louder than words." Anna rammed her hands onto her hips, pressing her white gown to her figure. "That is what I know."

He stared at his bride of only a few moments, at her narrowed eyes and furious red-cheeked face. A face he'd once woken up each morning eager to see. Lips he'd longed to make smile, longed to kiss. A few years had turned her from a girl to a woman. He could see it in the shape of her cheekbones and the spill of her hair, loose now, the way he'd always fantasized about seeing it, but had only once…in a stable…a long time ago.

"I don't remember," he said, "you telling me to stop in the garden when—"

"How dare you bring that up." Her cheeks flamed further. "I am referring to you not standing up to your mother, for not protecting my mother." She jabbed her finger his way. "I couldn't have cared less what happened to me after…" Her words trailed off.

He wanted to finish the sentence for her. After she'd been caught with her hand down his breeches rubbing his cock. But he sensed that would ignite the situation considerably.

"Well, isn't this adorable," Mrs. Dove-Lyon said. "Sparks are flying already. This truly is a match made in Heaven."

"More like Hell." Anna folded her arms and spun away, showing him her back. "And I am not going anywhere with him. As far as I am concerned, I am still a single maiden."

"Ah, but that is not true, and that is most certainly not what is going to happen." The Black Widow's voice had dropped low to a tone that commanded attention and obedience. "You are now Mrs. Frank Webb, Viscountess De-Wold, and you will act as such. And a woman of your status does not belong in a gambling house, oh no, you will leave right now with your husband and commence a new life ensuring you are loyal, dutiful, and willing in every way. For your husband is of a fine line and will wish to continue it with sons of his own, am I not right, my lord?"

Frank hesitated. His brain hadn't got that far ahead. Yes, they were man and wife, so that meant…God what he'd have done to have Anna in his bed a few years ago. He'd have done a deal with the devil himself, paid any price, including handing over his soul. But now. Now she wasn't willing, not to go with him, not to look at him, speak with him, not willing in any way as far as he could see.

Will that change?

"Loyal, dutiful, and willing," Anna said quietly and turned to face him. "Loyalty and duty I can do, I've done that all my life, but as for willing, that is not something that can be tricked out of someone, or bought, it must come from deep within, and I'm afraid, I know now, that deep within me, I am not willing and never will be." She paused. "Though that will not stop me being dutiful in the marital bed."

Frank scowled, his forehead creasing so much his eyebrows dropped low.

Anna opened her mouth to continue, but a bell rang in the corner.

"Ah, that will be your coach driver, my lord," Helena said. "Would you like me to ask him to wait around the back?"

"No." Frank reached for Anna's hand and grasped it before she could snatch it away. He held it tight. "My wife and I are leaving."

The first utterance of those words should have been special, sacred. *My wife and I.* But they weren't. They dragged over his tongue the same way he was now all but dragging Anna to the front door of the Lyon's Den.

When they reached it, he kept hold of her for fear she might bolt into the maze of streets that lined The Mall.

"Good day, sir," one of the bouncers said.

Frank managed a grunt as he all but bundled Anna into the sleek black coach. An especially stately vehicle with scarlet details and his family crest emblazed on the door. Two dapple gray mares were at the helm.

"I need my luggage." Anna sat heavily and folded her arms.

"Already stowed, my lady," the driver said, closing the door.

"My lady," she muttered.

"You should get used to it." Frank took a seat opposite her, glad that the noise of the street had faded now the coach door was closed, and they'd lost the curious eyes of the Lyon's Den.

"I will never get used to it."

"Anna." He leaned forward, elbows on his thighs, then braced as they began to move. "This wasn't my idea. I didn't know it was you I was playing for, that it was you I was marrying." He shook his head. "That it was you beneath the veil. Your face was impossible to see."

"As I had no idea it was you beneath that awful mask, though I have to say it was a good choice for you." She glared at him. "The devil also had no morals."

He bit on his bottom lip.

"Do you think Mrs. Dove-Lyon planned this?" she asked. "To put us together knowing our past."

"I don't know how she could have rigged the game. I won it fair and square."

She was quiet for a moment. "Did she know it was you playing?"

"I have no idea. I put the mask on before arriving on the gaming floor as I was instructed to." He thought back to the evening before. "It was several winning hands that got me to the center table, a lot of variables for me to not be there. But only one variable for you to be there, on that balcony, awaiting a husband."

"It was not my choice to wed. My mother, God rest her soul, paid Mrs. Dove-Lyon to find me a husband. She feared very much after the scandal at…at your home in Staffordshire that I'd never wed. Her biggest fear was for me to be a spinster, her dying wish was for me to marry."

"How much did she pay the Black Widow?"

"That is none of your business."

"I guess it isn't, but…"

"But what?"

They were rattling along now, over the cobbles, gaining on his townhouse in Mayfair. "My father gave your mother a generous severance pay, and I wonder if she ever told you that I—"

"That you what?"

"That I doubled it. I sent it on the next week."

Anna narrowed her eyes at him. "No, she never told me that."

"So, you see," he said, searching for signs of her softening. There were none. "I am not a man of no morals. My conscience acted."

"Your conscience, that is it exactly, my lord, you acted to ease your own guilt. It had nothing to do with mine or my mother's wellbeing. You simply wanted to sleep better at night."

"You really think I've slept better all of these years?"

"I couldn't give an owl's hoot how you've slept." She turned away and stared out of the window. "How long until we arrive?"

He beat down the anger that was growing in him. Had she no idea how much it had hurt him to never see her again? He'd been obsessed with her during those heady summer months of French tutoring. She was all he could think of. His teenage heart beating only for her and his body reacting just at the thought of hers.

"Not long now," he said. "I will organize a wedding breakfast for us."

"I'm not hungry."

"You need to eat."

She said nothing, and the stubborn line of her mouth told him there was likely to be good food going to waste.

CHAPTER EIGHT

"**W**HOA! WHOA!"

The coach pulled to a halt, and Anna regarded her new home through the window.

Before her was a lofty, red-bricked townhouse separated from the road by pointed black railings. It was four stories with ten large sash windows, all densely curtained, and a black front door that rivaled the gloss on the railings. It was the tallest in the row, the chimney pots reaching for the blue sky that did not match Anna's dark mood.

"Shall we?" Frank said when the footman opened the door.

She didn't reply. Instead, she simply moved past him and stepped down to the pavement. Her heart was thudding, her blood hot, though she was sure this did not show on her face as Frank alighted and stood alongside her.

"I'm sure you'll find it to your pleasing."

"What does that mean?"

"Simply that it is a very elegant home."

"And I am not used to such."

"That is not what I meant." He frowned and walked up to the front door.

Anna watched his familiar swagger. Time had not taken the edge off his confident walk, nor stooped his shoulders or fattened his waist. He was still a fine example of a gentleman.

But that didn't detract from what he'd done. Abandoned her and left her alone in her shame.

Glancing left, then right, she made a sudden decision. This wouldn't be her new home and he wouldn't be her new husband. The whole situation was ridiculous. More than that, it was abhorrent.

A sudden surge of energy rushed into her system. Hoisting her gown almost to her knees, she burst into a run, heading east, for that was where she knew best. Her feet slapped onto the hot pavement, her hair slipped from its pins, and she didn't allow herself to look back.

"Anna!"

Darn him!

"Wait!"

The end of the street was in view. She dodged a maid walking a small white dog, then took a left. Before her was a park, and she dashed over the road.

A noise behind her. Loud footsteps. "Anna, in the name of the good Lord, stop."

"No. Stay away from me." She entered the park and made toward the shade of a sprawling oak. She passed a group of nannies on a bench, prams parked in front of them as they chatted.

Perhaps he'd give up now. He wouldn't want to make a scene.

Suddenly a tightness caught her around the waist. In a sudden snapping motion, she was drawn to a halt and collided with what felt like a brick wall.

Except it wasn't a brick wall; it was Frank's hard body.

"Strewth, woman, what are you doing?"

"Get off me."

"No. And stop wriggling."

She was squirming and dragging at his arms around her. She threw her head back and caught him on the jaw.

"Blazes!" he swore. "Stop this now."

"Leave me be. I want no part of this sham marriage."

"It is not a sham. It is fully legal, and I intend to…"

"To what?"

"Never mind." His breath was hot beside her ear. "But you're coming with me. To our marital home."

"I have no desire to do anything of the sort and I…oh!"

He'd spun her around to face him, and in less time than it took a heart to beat, he'd stooped and dug his shoulder into her abdomen. The next thing she knew, the world was turned upside down, and she was rising into the air.

"Put me down. This instant." She clutched at his jacket and kicked at his gripping hands.

But that got her nowhere. In fact, it made the situation entirely worse, for he clasped his wide palm over her buttocks, pinning her to him, then began to stride back toward the street.

She gasped. Her cheeks flushing with burning heat. The nannies would be gossiping about this disreputable scene for months. It would spread through the servants' quarters of every house for miles around.

"Good afternoon to you, ladies," Frank said as he passed the nannies, acting for all the world like he didn't have a runaway bride hoisted over his shoulder.

She grunted in frustration, kicked at him again, and wished she hadn't gone so dizzy from being upside down. The path was a blur as he strode along it, the grass a fuzz of green in her peripheral vision. It was hard to catch her breath.

Much quicker than she'd expected, she spotted the wheels of the coach and the horses' hooves.

"I demand you…put…me…down."

"And have to chase you again, I think not." He tightened his grip on her behind.

Shame rushed through her.

"This wasn't quite how I'd intended to carry my bride over the threshold, but things don't always go to plan, isn't that right?"

He didn't deserve an answer, and her lips twisted into a grimace as the threshold passed beneath them.

The door shut with a resounding thud.

"My lord, you are home." A male voice that held confusion beneath its formality.

"Indeed, I am, Bannister," Frank said.

"And you have…company?"

"Not just any company, this is my new bride."

Before Bannister could comment, Anna found herself being lowered to her feet. She straightened. Dizziness besieged her again, a black fog creeping into her vision. Staggering to the right, she reached out to balance herself.

She needn't have bothered. Frank caught her around the waist, pulling her close.

"Get off me…" She touched her temple.

"Oh, my word, should I get the salts?" Bannister asked.

"Yes, good idea. I'll take her to the drawing room."

"Should she not lie down?"

"She'll be right as rain in a moment, it's just been an eventful morning."

"I'll say," Anna muttered, but then let Frank steer her through a doorway to her right.

He gently encouraged her sit on a plush, emerald green wingback chair, then stood before her, hands on his hips, coat tails caught behind them. "That was quite the scene."

"It wouldn't have been if you hadn't chased me."

"And be left by my bride on our wedding day. What kind of man do you take me for?"

"A man who was happy to leave me to carry the burden of something *we* did together."

"You were well compensated."

"Is that all you thought it would take?" Her vision had settled, the lightheadedness receding.

"What do you mean?"

"If you have to ask, then you don't deserve to know."

He pursed his lips, and a crease marred his brow, she'd never noticed that before.

"I need a drink." He turned and strode to the drinks trolley complete with several decanters holding amber liquid. He sloshed a few inches into a crystal glass and drank deep.

Great. He's dipping rather deep on the alcohol now, too.

"My lord, I have some of your mother's smelling salts." Bannister walked into the room holding a small silver gilded bottle in the shape of a heart. He offered it to Frank.

"I am quite well now." Anna held up her hand. "That won't be necessary." Smelling salts had never appealed to her, and the thought of using his mother's, even worse.

"She hasn't quite colored up, my lord."

"Yes, but if she doesn't want them." He poured once again. "Oh, leave them there, I will insist if necessary."

"Of course." Bannister set the salts on the polished table. "Can I get you anything else, my lord?"

"No."

"Will that be all?"

"Yes, thank you. No wait," Frank said. "We wish to have a wedding breakfast."

"For how many guests, my lord?"

"Er…" He looked at Anna. "Two."

Bannister hesitated, then, "I will set Cook to it."

"It won't be necessary." Anna held up her hand.

"It absolutely will be necessary." Frank frowned at her. "We will eat within the hour. I, for one, am quite famished. And Bannister, see that Lady Anna's belongings are taken upstairs to the bedchamber."

"Which bedchamber, my lord?" Bannister looked between Anna and Frank.

"The one adjoining mine," Frank snapped. "Naturally."

"Of course, my lord, certainly, my lord." He left the room.

Anna straightened her back and knotted her fingers together. Silence descended.

Frank walked to the window and stared out at the street, still nursing his drink.

He cut a fine figure, and for a moment, Anna was transported back to their school room in Staffordshire. Whenever he'd looked out at the De-Wold estate, she'd admired his back view. His clothes had clung to him in a way that had made her want to know what lay beneath. To learn the shape of his muscles, the width of his shoulders in palm lengths, the feel of his buttocks beneath her hands.

She flushed and looked away. That wasn't a train of thought she had any intention of entertaining. Frank Webb, Viscount De-Wold, her husband. It was simply the most laughable day ever, if it weren't so damn annoying.

The mantel clock ticked. A child wailed in its pram as it was pushed beneath the window, hopefully heading home for feed time. A dog barked, so did another, a rowdy conversation.

Still, they were silent.

Until eventually, Bannister came back into the room. "The wedding breakfast is served."

"Excellent." Frank smacked down his glass and held out his hand to Anna. "Shall we?"

She didn't take his hand. Why they hell should she when she'd had no choice but to be here? Surely a sane man would have let her escape. Who on God's earth wanted an unwilling, unhappy, uncooperative bride?

Frank didn't say anything further as she stood and walked from the room.

Bannister was eyeing her curiously. Likely he'd had a grilling from the other staff. No doubt shocked to hear their master had taken a bride so suddenly and desperate to know who she was, and even more curious as to why.

Anna paused. "I take it we haven't met," she said to Bannister.

"No, my lady, should we have?"

"Perhaps if you'd been at the De-Wold's country residence you might recall."

"Ah I see." He nodded. "But no, I only serve the Webb family here in London."

Anna didn't reply. It was only a matter of time until he found out she was the former governess's daughter. The *bird of paradise* who had been caught with her hand down the pants of the future Viscount De-Wold. And then what would he say? If he was looking at her with curiosity laced with suspicion now, he'd be condemning her once he knew the sordid truth.

She headed swiftly into the room opposite the drawing room, the open door telling her it held a large dining table.

"A most excellent spread conjured at such short notice," Frank said, pulling out a chair on a long dark walnut table surrounded by at least eleven more chairs with brass, paw like-feet. The surface was so polished, it reflected the ornate ceiling decorated with murals and two overly large candelabras, each candle lit despite the lightness of the hour.

Anna sat. Before her were a selection of plates. Buttered toast, tongue, ham, eggs, honey cake, and apple tart, and to wash it down, drinking chocolate.

Frank took a seat at the head of the table, a similar selection of plates before him. She could barely see him around the candelabras.

"Open a bottle of our finest Madeira from the cellar," Frank said with a click of his fingers. "We are celebrating, are we not?"

Anna held in a huff. In the vast room, being watched over by portraits of stern ancestors and feeling hot and itchy in her gown, it was more like a wake...her wake.

"We *are* celebrating, Anna," Frank repeated. "I only intend to marry once, and that day is today."

"Certainly, my lord." Bannister looked between them, then made a sharp exit.

"A wedding breakfast is supposed to have guests," Anna remarked. "Not one person on the face of this earth is going to be pleased that we are married."

"So, you are willing to accept this marriage?"

"You do not care what the staff will say? What society will say...?" She paused. "Your mother?"

"No, Anna, I do not care. I do not care one bit."

"You did once upon a time." She tilted her chin.

"We must—" He balled his hand and put it on the table, he didn't slam it down, but just the action showed his irritation was growing. "We must put that...incident behind us." He narrowed his eyes.

"Incident, is that what you call it?"

"Anna, I wanted you and you wanted me. Why is it different now? What is different now?"

How could he even think such a thing? There was no want between them. "Oh, you are such a..."

"What...? Pray tell. Don't hold your tongue, bride of mine."

"You are such a pompous, misguided fool," she almost spat the words. "Of course it is different now. While you have been cavorting around Europe, bedding lady-bird women, striking deals worth hundreds, or make that thousands of pounds, I have lived in disgrace, nursed a sick mother, mourned, then worked in an establishment of questionable income and—"

"And what did you do there?" He tilted his chin and placed the tips of both his index fingers on the point.

"Whatever do you mean?" She rubbed her locket.

"What did you do while working for the Black Widow?" His voice was low. Dark. Dangerous almost. His eyes narrowed further, turning them into thin slits.

"Not what you're thinking." She sniffed. "I told you once that I wanted to be a virgin on my wedding day, and I am." She bit on her bottom lip. For this was her wedding day, and as her husband, Frank would no doubt lay claim to her virginity. What was more, she'd just laid the fact right there on the table.

"I am pleased to hear it," he said, reaching for a hunk of bread and tearing at it. He slathered it in butter. "For I always hoped to marry a virgin."

"Yet, you were so keen to take my virtue when we were not wed."

"I was young, caught up in the moment, it was as if you and I were the only people in the world and—" He quieted as Bannister entered the room carrying an uncorked bottle.

"For lord *and* lady?" Bannister asked.

"Indeed." Frank reached for his glass and held it aloft.

Bannister filled it to the rim. He then half-filled Anna's.

"Thank you," Frank said. "I will not need you again until morn. Please take the day off."

"But, my lord, it is still broad daylight and your jacket and—"

"I wish to spend the day with my new wife, undisturbed, and we have sufficient food and wine here."

Bannister hesitated then, "Are you quite sure, my lord?"

"I said as such." Frank flicked his hand toward the door. "Please. Take leave."

"Very well. As you wish." Bannister left the room.

"Please, eat, Anna." Frank took a sip of his drink. "It is clear Cook has gone to a lot of trouble."

She reached for a slice of ham. "And is it Mrs. Flora? The cook here?"

"Mrs. Flora?"

"The cook from your country estate? The one with the mole." Anna pointed to her top lip.

"No, here we have separate staff as Bannister already told you. But why…?" He set down his glass. "Ah, I see, she was there that day. She saw us."

"And failed to keep her mouth shut as your mother requested. The shame her gossip brought made my mother all the sicker."

"For that I am sorry."

"And is she still in employment at the De-Wold estate in Stafford-shire."

"Indeed, she is, but as the new lady of the house, Anna, you are free to dismiss her."

"Lady of the house," she scoffed. "I don't think so."

"But of course you are." He stared straight at her. "As of this very day, you are Anna Webb, the Viscountess De-Wold. Mistress of a vast estate and elegant townhouse. That is something you need to get used to."

CHAPTER NINE

FRANK STUDIED HIS bride as she sat with her back to him, staring out of the window at the darkening street and the park beyond. She'd been sullen all afternoon. He'd almost have preferred it if she'd quarreled with him. At least that way he'd have been entertained. As it was, he'd read *The Morning Post* twice, reports of the King Regent's excesses entertaining both him and the satirical artists.

"Would you like to play the piano?" he asked, breaking the long silence.

"I don't play."

"A game of whist?"

"No, thank you."

"A game of checkers?"

"You do not need to entertain me, Frank."

He liked the way she said his name, even if it was tainted with her obvious annoyance at the situation. "I am not saying I do."

"I have managed without you for many years, remember."

He stood and walked over to her, stopped at her side, and looked out of the window. "And now we are together again, leg-shackled, whether either of us like it or not."

"You did not have to go through with the wedding."

"Neither did you."

She frowned up at him. "Actually, I did."

Now he was curious. "How come?"

"My mother paid Mrs. Dove-Lyon to find me a husband. It was her dying wish that I marry well and secure my future."

Now it was making sense to Frank. The Anna he knew was strong-willed, independent, confident. Her going through with the anonymous marriage had puzzled him, though it had all happened so fast, he'd barely had time to pause and think about it himself. "In which case, you should be pleased that your mother's dying wish has been fulfilled."

"I really don't think she'd be happy that it is *you,* of all people, I have wed." She folded her arms tight over her chest, scooping the soft rise of her breasts upward, the neck line of her gown pressing into her pale flesh.

Frank tore his eyes away from the locket sitting at her cleavage. Her gentle curves had tormented his teenage self. Back then, he'd laid in the privacy of his bedchamber imagining what lay beneath her clothing. Grown hard as he'd thought of touching her, exploring, tasting, claiming. He'd wanted Anna like he'd never wanted any woman before or since.

He cleared his throat. "On the contrary, I think she would be happy, for surely our marriage simply proves that what we had back then was real. Destiny had mapped our path as one, and we simply stumbled upon it too early."

"What nonsense you talk." She clicked her tongue on the roof of her mouth. A cute gesture she'd done in French classes that he'd long forgotten about, but now remembered. Although on this day it wasn't French grammar that was irritating her…it was him.

"What would you like to do before nightfall?" he asked, trying to steer the subject into more civilized territory. "It is getting late for a stroll, but we could get some air in the rear courtyard."

"I do not wish to stroll or get air anywhere with you." She stood.

"Are you hungry?" His jaw tensed as he looked her up and down.

"I am not. We have had quite the spread."

"Can I get you some wine?" He gestured to the decanter.

"No. I should like to read. I'd imagine you have a library within this grand townhouse."

"Indeed, I have." He gestured to the door. "And I am sure you will not be disappointed."

She didn't answer but followed him from the room.

Frank led her up the main stairwell, sliding his hand on the polished banister and wondering what his father, grandfather, and great grandfather would think of the unusual way in which he'd sourced a bride. Their large portraits, each shown standing in front of the De-Wold house and wearing formal dress, gave nothing away.

At the top of the staircase, he turned right, past a bow fronted sideboard decorated atop with two porcelain vases stuffed full of pink roses and a mahogany chair with gold thread running through its cushion.

"In here," he said, pushing open a heavy door.

The library faced the rear of the house, and heavy swagged drapes, also shot through with gold thread, partially obscured the two lead-paned windows. Every bit of wall space was lined with shelving with the exception of a large marble fireplace that held above it a portrait of his great aunt in an elegant white gown. In the center of the room, a long-polished, claw-footed table was set with brass-based lamps.

Frank stepped in and waited until Anna had done the same. He closed the door.

The familiar, still-aired silence surrounded him, though today there was a tightness to it. Anna's frostiness contracting his muscles and creating a knot between his shoulder blades. "I trust you will find something to your liking."

"I'm sure I will." She peered at a set of red-leather-bound books, seemingly reading the titles.

"Though you have been known to be rather picky."

"What do you mean?" she asked.

"I sent you a letter once, Anna." He was unable to keep the accusatory tone from his voice. "Remember?"

"You passed me many letters between our tutorial tables."

"No. They were notes." He curled his hands over the back of an oak chair that sat at the head of the table. "Once I sent you a letter."

"Did you?"

Irritation clawed at his scalp. For a second, he'd returned to the moment of being handed his unopened letter. *Au Revoir.* "Yes. I did. And if you'd opened it, you'd perhaps recall the contents."

She said nothing. Instead, she pulled a book from the shelf and carefully began to read the first page.

"Anna."

Nothing.

"Anna, listen to me."

"What if I don't want to listen to you?" She snapped the book closed and turned to face him.

"That is not relevant." He tapped his chest. "I am your husband now, and you *will* listen to me." He paused. He didn't want to say the next words because he knew they'd stoke the fire of her temper, but the fact of the matter was he'd become her husband. "You *will* obey me."

"Huh. You always did insist on being obeyed."

"What is that supposed to mean?" Damn and blast it.

She looked so sweet standing in his library with a shard of evening light glancing off her dress and catching in her hair. The last thing he wanted to do was argue with her like this. She'd been his first love, the one who'd gotten away, and now she was back. He'd been looking for her, and failing, in every woman he'd been with since. He wanted to take her in his arms and never let her go. But he couldn't, not with the pain of her rejection humming through his veins and the way she appeared ready to claw him like an angered cat or worse, kick him like a feisty mare.

"Oh, you might have pretended we were friends, Frank, but you always were the one to get the last say. *Persuade* me to obey you."

"That is not true."

"You know it is."

"Give me one example." He held out his palms. "Just one."

She was quiet for a moment, the book held like a shield before her chest. "I told you we shouldn't kiss, yet you did it anyway."

"You kissed me back."

"I was young and foolish."

"As was I, but that didn't stop us from having feelings for each other. Of being able to think of nothing but each other from dawn to dusk and then haunt one another's dreams each and every night."

"Now that I am older and wiser, I know exactly what you were thinking of, dreaming of, Frank. That is something I have learned about men whilst at the Lyon's Den. Their thoughts are ruled by what is in their breeches."

Her words were like a punch to the gut. How could she think that? He'd been wholly in love with her. It was the only explanation for the heartache he'd felt when she'd left. "Women also have desires of the flesh." He stepped closer to her. "I am also older and wiser and know that only too well."

"I'm sure you do." She raised her left eyebrow and held his gaze.

Damn it. This wasn't going how he wanted it to. His bedchamber experiences in Paris were the last thing he intended to debate. "Why didn't you open the letter?"

"Because you were out of my life, and I wanted it to stay that way…forever."

"It was not a letter about the weather and my health," he said.

"I do not care what it was about."

Frank ignored her indifferent shrug. "I wanted to inform you of my father's sudden death. I was struggling to come to terms with the fact I hadn't even had a chance to say my goodbyes, telling you, perhaps seeing you, it felt like it would help with my grief." He paused, hoping she might say something. She didn't. "And my mother. She barely paused in the endless stream of possible brides for me. None of whom were you, so none of whom I could entertain marrying."

"You didn't really want to marry me." She tipped her head, then pulled her lips in on themselves as if holding in words.

"I wanted to see you. I wanted to make amends. My position was different after my father died. I was the new Viscount De-Wold, free to make my own decisions without consequence. I could marry whom I wanted."

"Your mother is still alive. Your mother still hates me. She would never have allowed it."

"I respect my mother very much, but I am not beholden to the future she wants for me." He was aware of his voice deepening, echoing around the lofty library. "I always held the belief that my wife would be of my choosing."

"Except you didn't choose me. It was a twist of fate at the hand of the Black Widow, remember."

"Anna." He moved closer and set his hands on her shoulders. He felt the delicate shape of her body and the heat of her skin through her gown. "You are the woman I have always wanted for my wife. From the moment I first saw you I have..."

"You have what?"

He could make out a few freckles on her nose that hadn't been there before and a flash of wildness in her eyes he'd seen many times. "I have always loved you, Anna. I have loved you from the moment I first saw you on the carriage park at the estate."

Suddenly, she set her hand on his chest and shoved.

He took a stunned step backward.

"Stop talking twaddle." She slammed the book onto the table so hard the spine creaked. "You don't love me. You have never loved me. If you had, you wouldn't have seen my mother and I thrown onto the streets." She pointed outside. "But now, as it happens, that's where I'd prefer to be rather in this stuffy big house with you."

"You don't mean that." Heat flared on his cheeks. He'd just professed his love. Bared his heart and soul, and she was throwing it back at him as if swatting away a fly.

"I do." She rammed her hands onto her hips. "Because this marriage is a sham and will never work."

"It damn well will work." He'd spoken through gritted teeth.

"How can it?"

"The boot is quite on the other leg. This marriage is legally binding, you signed the goddamn register as did our witnesses. You are stuck with me as your husband, Anna, me…as your husband."

She dragged in a breath, her jaw tight, her eyes narrow. "Where is my bedchamber? I wish to retire for the night."

CHAPTER TEN

ANNA PICKED UP a small golden bird and examined the exquisite detail of the feathered wings. She then placed it back on the dresser, which had already been laid with her meager toiletries and hairbrush along with her pressed bluebell in its frame. Behind the flower, secreted away, she still had her faded, clandestinely passed notes from Frank.

Neither she nor her tattered possessions belonged in such a lavish bedchamber. Beautiful as it was, it just felt wrong. All her life her home had been akin to servant quarters, used mattresses, small high windows, threadbare rugs—if any.

Yet here she was, standing alone in what had just been referred to, by Frank, as her new bedchamber.

It was vast and had an enormous window looking out over the park with golden drapes so heavy she wondered if she'd ever be able to draw them. The four-poster bed had a domed ceiling with two ornate doves atop and rose gold curtains held back by thickly roped swags. A dado rail around the center of the room separated pale green lower walls from green and white floral paper above. Several darkly framed paintings of landscapes, flowers, and birds adorned the walls. A harp stood in one corner, a pale blue Sheraton arm chair in another, and two lamps appeared to guard a fireplace which was lit despite the summer month. On the mantel, a gilded swan, wings spread, reflected in an elaborately decorative mirror.

The veiled hat sat on a table beside a wardrobe. She pulled open the door and found her small collection of clothes carefully hung within.

She reached for her nightgown, pale pink from many washes, and walked toward a basin on a stand. The water was warm, and she set about washing, peering warily at the door. Not the one she'd come through, but the one Frank had disappeared wordlessly through. She guessed it was his bedchamber. The luxury of wealth, meaning married couples could have their own space. Something in this instance she was incredibly grateful for.

She quickly readied herself for bed with lavender soap and powder and cold cream. She left her hair in its long taut plait. It was not the wedding night she'd hoped for. At one time in her life, she couldn't imagine being touched by anyone other than Frank. Yet right now, she was too angry with him. Angry that he'd got his way, that he had power over her as her husband. That he still said things that were untrue.

Carefully, she folded her gown over the chair next to the harp. Outside, London had turned dark, and on the street below the lamplighters were at work with ladders and long poles.

She closed her eyes and an image of Frank, young Frank, how she used to see him, filled her mind. His smile had been infectious, his touch addictive, and when he'd been in a room, he was all she could see, all she could think about.

There'd never been anyone else who had affected her that way. No one who could make her heart trip over itself. Steal her dreams. Catch her breath. There had only ever been Frank.

And now it seemed there only ever would be Frank.

No, surely, he would seek an annulment. His mother would persuade him to do as such the instant she found out about the marriage.

Quickly, she opened her eyes, banishing his image. If she allowed herself to think of him as hers, as her husband for even a moment, she was opening herself up to heartbreak all over again. Once was bad enough, twice she wasn't sure she'd survive.

Suddenly the door to Frank's bedchamber opened, and he stepped through to her room, wearing only low-slung breeches.

Her breath caught. He was no longer a young man, but broader across the chest and shoulders, his body hair thicker especially the line that ran from navel to waistband, and with an even more determined glint in his eyes.

Quickly she turned back to the window. He was so damn handsome, his body one sculptors would die to capture in stone.

As she fought for breath, he stepped close behind her, very close, his soap and spice scent filling her lungs.

She waited for him to speak, to feel his warm breath beside her ear.

He would instruct her to undress. Lay on the bed. Open herself for him. That was what she'd heard happened on wedding nights. It was the way of the world, the way of marriage…the way babies were made. Or in Frank's case, heirs.

But he didn't utter a word, nor did he touch her. He stood silently as if breathing in her powdery scent.

Her stomach did a strange flip as heat from his chest spread onto her back. Her traitorous body remembering his touch of long ago. Coming back to life at the thought of those stolen caresses.

His knuckles brushed her nape.

She sucked in a breath and closed her eyes. Instantly back in the stable, Diamond watched as Frank delicately unraveled her braid.

He was doing the same again. Working his way up her long hair and freeing the strands.

A conversation of years ago flooded her memory…

"It is beautiful loose like this," he murmured. *"You should wear it this way always."*

"My mother would not allow it."

"If I were your husband, I would insist upon it. In the bedchamber, at least, I would want my wife's hair free and swishing around her body and over mine."

She balled her hands into fists and pressed her legs together, heat spreading in her most private place.

He intended her to have loose hair as he consummated their marriage—when he took her virginity. Nerves warred with an infuriating longing. Frustration vied with desire.

How could this be happening? How had she ended up in this situation with Frank? Out of all the men in the world it had to be him beneath the devil's mask.

And a devil he was for making her feel this way. Wanting him. Hating him.

He reached the base of her neck, his fingertips tickling over her nape as he fanned out her hair.

Goose bumps spread over her scalp, her shoulders, and it was all she could do to suppress a quiver of longing—longing for more. Longing to tell him exactly what she thought of him for touching her this way. As if not a moment had passed since they'd been in the stable.

He ran his fingers through her hair, like a comb, running down her back to where it stopped midway.

She could still hear his breathing, slow and steady and deep. A strange white-hot sensation had flooded her body. Her breasts were heavy and her nipples ached they were so tight.

He pressed in close behind her, chest to her back, and set his hands on her shoulders.

This was it, she was sure. Now he'd undress her. Spread her legs and put his thick hardness deep inside her until seed was spilled.

And as his wife, it was her duty to take him.

She tensed. The fighter in her wanted to object, yet the hot-blooded woman in her wanted it all, everything…all of him.

She remained still. Afraid to move. Afraid to break the spell.

Frank slid his fingers beneath the elastic holding the right puffed sleeve of her nightgown. He slipped it, slowly, agonizingly slow, to the tip of her shoulder and left it hovering at the point that it might slip down.

In the reflection in the window, his head appeared next to hers. For a moment he caught her gaze, then he closed his eyes and dipped his head, pressing his lips to the bare flesh on the curve between her neck and her shoulder.

She gasped. The sensation of his warm lips on her skin was so utterly thrilling. He'd always had the ability to make the rest of the world retreat and this was no exception. "Frank," she said breathlessly.

He lifted his head and touched his lips to the shell of her ear.

A tremor went through her, one she couldn't dampen. She had to lock her knees to stay upright.

"You should know," he whispered, then left his words hanging.

"What?" she managed.

Very gently, he tugged her sleeve up, covering the patch of skin that still tingled from his kiss. "That I only wish to bed a willing wife."

She stared straight ahead. Her vision blurring as she studied her own reflection with Frank so close.

"But you will be," he went on, "before long, you will be begging me to take your precious virginity and you will enjoy every moment of it. That is a promise I make here, now, to you."

Suddenly he stepped away. His heat and touch leaving her.

Pressing a hand to her chest, she spun around but was greeted with his departing figure as he paced to the door. The last she saw of him was his broad muscular back as he slipped into his bedchamber and was gone.

"Oh, dear Lord above." She staggered to the bed and sat heavily. What had he just done to her? Her body barely felt like her own. It was as if hot pepper had been rubbed over her skin, starting in the spot he'd kissed and headed to her nape and down her spine. It went lower, lower still and between her legs. Insistent humming like a musical chord. She felt hot and wet and swollen down there and tugged up her nightgown, pressing her fingers to the neediest spot.

Biting her lip to hold in a groan, she rubbed herself. Something she'd done before when thinking of Frank. Only this time, it was so much more intense because she could still feel his touch, smell him, and his erotic words rang in her ears.

Speeding up, she curled her toes on the rug and dropped her head back, her hair swishing behind her. What she needed was relief. A quick burst of pleasure to take the edge off her confusing, maddening need for a man who had tortured her heart all that time ago.

The pressure built quickly, reaching a point where she knew stopping wasn't an option. She hoped to dear God Frank didn't walk in and see her now—the shame would be unbearable.

With the tips of her fingers rotating over her nub, she held in her desperate pants. Just a little bit more and she'd tip over the edge. Give her body what it longed for.

And then it was there, a lovely, swift climax that burst from her core and spread over her skin. Her inner muscles spasmed, heated and dampened, and she closed her eyes and allowed bright sparks to flood her vision.

But as soon as the bliss arrived it abated, diminishing quickly and leaving only a morsel of satisfaction behind.

Pushing at her nightgown to cover her modesty, she sucked in a breath and stared again at the dark window. She was thankful there was no house opposite to see into her second-floor window. It hadn't even been a thought before she'd touched herself, which just made her madder at Frank. He still had the power to consume her to the point of insanity.

FRANK SHUT THE door between his bedchamber and his new wife's, with the taste of her still on his lips. A delicate, long remembered mix of lavender and powder and something sweetly erotic that his body craved.

"Damn it," he muttered, leaning back on the wooden door and closing his eyes.

What he really wanted to do was go in there and claim her. Consummate their marriage. Do what they'd both longed to do all those years ago in the stable. If they'd hadn't been rudely interrupted by the stable boys and the gamekeeper, he'd have taken them both to a place of extreme pleasure, one they'd never have forgotten.

But they had been interrupted. They had been sent their separate ways. Love and lust had turned to anger and rejection.

He rubbed his temples; they throbbed the way his cock did. Standing so close to her, in a quiet, private bedchamber, knowing he could sink deep into her body, had every right to, had made his blood heat and desire rage.

Frank wasn't the kind of man to take what wasn't given. He wanted, no make that needed, Anna to desire him the way he desired her. And that would happen, he just wasn't sure how or when.

He took a step forward, but it was damn uncomfortable. "Blast it." He stooped a little and turned to the door, placed the flat of one palm upon it. With the other hand, he shoved at the fold in his breeches, releasing his erection.

He took it in his fist and began to work himself vigorously. There was only one thing for it, he'd have to bring himself relief.

As he masturbated, his balls tightened, and he recalled doing the very same thing after several French classes with Anna's name on his lips and her smiling face hovering in his mind's eye.

He'd wanted her then as he wanted her now. She was the only woman he'd ever thought of when indulging in self-gratification. She was the only woman who hadn't been forthcoming with offering her body.

Oh, she would have done her duty, he was sure of that. Laid back, parted her thighs and no doubt thought of England as he'd stuck his cock into her.

But that wasn't enough for Frank. He wanted her lust to match his. Her body to react to his the way his would to hers. He wanted her kisses, her caresses, her post-coital, honey-sweet words of endearment.

And until he could get all of that, he'd sleep alone.

Gritting his teeth and tensing his belly, he sped up. His shaft was steely hard, the ache almost too painful to manage. He needed to find relief from his craving.

"Bugger and blazes," he gasped, his balls retracting as he reached his climax.

Holding in a groan, he swiped up a kerchief from the dresser at his side.

His seed surged up his cock, bringing with it the immense bliss of release. He bit on his bottom lip to hold in a string of further curse words and imagined he was inside Anna, feeling her orgasm around his cock as she, too, succumbed.

With a guttural moan that vibrated from his chest and through his throat, he flooded the kerchief, once, twice, three times. It was not what he'd planned for his wedding night, a night that should have been the start of his ambition to create heirs. But Anna was also not the wife he thought he'd have, which left him little choice but to do nothing more than think of her as he orgasmed.

Something he was quite used to doing.

Chapter Eleven

"**D**ID YOU SLEEP well, my lady?"

Anna blinked and stared at the floral canopy above her. "Er, yes, thank you." Had she? She could barely remember, she'd been so tired. The night had simply been an expanse of blackness.

"Oh dear, dear, your curtains were not even pulled. Bannister told me you mustn't be disturbed for the entire day, but really…" The young maid set a tray on the bed. Laden with toast and preserves and cake. A single yellow flower peeked from a slim vase and a teapot decorated with delicate yellow flowers and had been placed next to a matching cup and saucer.

"Thank you." Anna pulled herself to sitting only to find the maid there in an instant fussing with her pillows.

Not used to such attention, Anna leaned forward to help.

"No, no, you're all set." The maid smiled. She was a young, early twenties, with curly hair the color of carrot peelings, and an expanse of freckles over her nose and cheeks. "I am Mary, your lady's maid."

"My lady's maid?"

Mary smiled. "We are so glad you're here. His lordship has been a long time finding a wife."

"He has been busy with the business, I suppose."

Mary nodded and went to the fire. She poked the dead embers. "I will have the housemaid come and relight this."

"It's fine. The morning appears quite warm." Anna reached for a slice of toast and spread butter on it.

"If you're sure. But it will be lit this evening, and I can assure you the curtains will be drawn." She bustled to the wardrobe. "What do you wish to wear today? Do you have plans?"

"Er, no, none that I am aware of."

Mary opened the cupboard door. "Mmm, your selection isn't very broad. Can I send for more from your parent's home perhaps?"

"No, that's not possible." Anna bit into the toast. She couldn't ever remember breakfasting in bed before.

"Oh?" Mary turned to her.

"My parents are dead."

"Lud, I am sorry to hear that."

"It was God's will."

Mary retrieved Anna's pale blue gown from the wardrobe. The base and the sleeves were embroidered with small flowers and butterflies. "How about this one?"

"Yes. Thank you." Anna was relieved that Mary had picked out the best gown she owned. "I think I must shop for some more. And some undergarments, I am rather low, indeed not even a corset at the moment."

"Some new clothing would be just the job, though this dress has a corset set within it." Mary smiled.

"That is true. It is the only one that has though."

"I could come with you, to the shop, if you would like."

"I would like that very much."

"Or better still." Mary set the gown on the chair beside the window. "I could have a selection of dresses and undergarments from Madam Boudiere's sent to the house for you to choose from. She is quite the seamstress."

"Yes, I have heard of her." Anna had admired her work for some time.

"And some hats from the Bow Street Milliner."

"That would be very helpful."

"I am here to be helpful." Mary smiled.

Anna liked her already.

"Anything I can do, just say the word."

"Some warm water perhaps, to bathe."

"I have already requested the bath tub be filled and can I suggest the jasmine soap bar, it really does have the most pleasing summery aroma."

"I adore jasmine, so yes, thank you."

Mary's smile widened. "The bath will be waiting in the room next door."

"Can I ask you one thing?"

"Of course, my lady."

"Where is Lady Webb?"

Mary appeared confused.

"I mean, where is Fra...Lord Webb's mother? The dowager. Is she here?"

"Ah, no, she left yesterday morn with Florence."

"Florence?"

"Her lap dog." Mary was quiet.

Anna knew what she was thinking. Why didn't the new Viscountess De-Wold know the whereabouts of her mother-in-law or that Florence was a dog. "It has been a whirlwind, this marriage," Anna said. "And I thank you for your support and discretion."

"Of course, my lady. I am here to serve not to gossip. I've never been fond of bandy words or Canterbury tales."

"A fine quality. Thank you."

Anna watched her lady's maid leave, her footsteps quiet and her movements efficient. Never in her life did she think she'd have a maid all to herself, to do her bidding, care for her. Would she ever get used to it? And more to the point, did she like it?

Two hours later, bathed and coifed and wearing a little rouge, Anna came down the wide staircase and entered the drawing room.

Frank was seated beside the window holding the newspaper. When he saw her, he set it aside and stood.

Anna stopped. Her heart doing a silly flip, the way it used to in the school room, just at the sight of him.

Wearing pale buckskin breeches, a white linen shirt, and a silken emerald-green waistcoat along with polished hessian boots cut to a point at the top of his shins, he certainly looked more mature than he had back then. But his expression, the way his attention instantly latched onto her...that was the same as all those years ago.

"I trust you slept well," he said, moving to a tray of tea.

"Yes, thank you."

"Would you like some?"

"I have just taken tea upstairs."

"Very well." He set the teapot down. "I, too, have just drunk."

Anna stepped past him to the window. She looked out at the street and park beyond.

He breathed deep. "You have changed your perfume."

"Yes. My lady's maid, Mary, she found it for me."

"I do not wish you to wear it again."

"I beg your pardon." She frowned at him.

He shrugged, and a smile tugged his lips. "It is the one my mother favors. I do not wish my wife to smell like my mother."

"Perhaps I could use that information to my advantage."

"And why would you want to do that?"

"I sense it repels you." She raised her eyebrows.

"It is rather off-putting." He tipped his head, studied her. "But is that really what you want? To repel me?"

She thought of the night before. When he'd cast a spell on her, kissing the curve of her shoulder, making her think of nothing but him. The way she'd had to satisfy her cravings herself when she knew he would have been able to do it much better. She swallowed tightly. "You know full well I do not wish to be in this marriage."

"But you are in this marriage in the eyes of the Lord, the law, and society." He gestured outside. "Come, we will take a walk beside the park lake. The fresh air will be a tonic for both of us."

"If that is what you insist upon for today."

"It is the start of things I plan for today, our first full day as a wedded couple." He withdrew a gold watch from his fob pocket and examined it.

"Do not expect too much. I will be sleeping alone again tonight."

"As you wish." He reached for a morning jacket and pulled it on. "Though do not think I have forgotten how you once yearned for my kisses." He lowered his voice. "How you pressed close to me, your breasts against my chest, your lips on mine, breaths coming fast, heart beating, wanting more, and—"

"That was another life time." Her cheeks heated. Irritation gnawed at her.

"It was only a few years ago, and I remember it so clearly." He flattened his jacket against his lean torso, brushing away a near invisible speck of fluff. "How you told me you saw me as just Frank. No one else had ever said that to me."

"I also told you that we could never marry. Society wouldn't allow it."

"Yet here we are. Married. Strange how life goes."

"Strange how you got your way." She huffed.

"I usually do." He crooked his arm so she could take his elbow. "Come. Let us get your shawl in case the day turns chilly."

Bannister saw them out the door, and they crossed the road, dodging a horse-drawn mail coach, and walked along the street into the park.

"I do not wish to see the nannies who witnessed me being hoisted over your shoulder," Anna said, glancing around. "That was humiliating and will likely be tittle-tattle all over Mayfair."

"If you had not run from me, you would not have been retrieved."

"Retrieved? I am not an animal."

He chuckled. "So don't act like one."

She huffed. "Whatever happened to your horse Diamond?"

"He took two second places at Royal Ascot and now lives a very happy life."

"What do you mean?"

"His only job is to cover mares."

"Cover mares?"

"Yes. Lucky old chap has one duty to fulfill, have lots of sex."

"Frank!"

He grinned and shrugged. "It is the way of horse breeding. When a bloodline is good, it is imperative to ensure plenty of stock in the same line. Champions sire champions."

"And he is at the De-Wold estate?"

"Yes. I am sure he will remember you."

They turned into the park and took the path in the opposite direction to the way she'd run the day before. "I doubt that."

"Horses have very good memories."

Anna watched a magpie hopping along a branch, carrying what appeared to be a bit of bread. "As does your mother. Good memory, that is."

"My mother?"

"Yes. What do you think she is going to say when she finds out about...this."

"About the new Viscountess De-Wold, you mean." He smiled, small lines shooting from the outer corners of his eyes.

"It is not funny. Your mother hates me."

"She does not."

"I beg to differ."

"Were you not there in the kitchen garden?" She couldn't keep the incredulity from her voice. "When she caught us...me...doing that, with you. I'm sure she would have had me hanged or stoned if she thought she'd get away with it."

"My mother has mellowed."

"I doubt that."

"Losing my father hit her hard."

"Yet from what you have told me, she never lost the energy to keep offering a supply of young women for you to choose from."

He paused. "That is true."

"So, what in God's name do you think she's going to say when she finds out about me?"

They began walking alongside the lake. A group of young boys played with paper boats in the shallows. Blowing them with straws in an apparently exciting race.

"I guess," Frank said, "we will find out when we go to the De-Wold estate at the end of the week."

"The end of the week?" She stopped under the cool canopy of a large oak tree and faced him. Dappled shadows scattered across his face and over his jacket. "No. We can't. Not so soon."

"She will see the announcement in the paper. The Black Widow was quite specific about posting it."

"I know, but...?"

"But what?"

Anna didn't reply.

"You think by then you will have run away again, Anna? That you will have sought an annulment?" He stepped closer, his eyebrows pulling low. "Is that really what you want?"

"How can you not want the same thing? You have no more desire to be wed to me than I you."

"How do you know that?"

"Because we were tricked into this. You, for one, were tap-hackled when you agreed to the card game."

"I was not, a few fine wines, nothing more."

"If you say so, but you cannot disagree you were hasty and imprudent when agreeing to take a wife as your prize."

"I am never imprudent." His tone was low and dark again.

Anna ignored the warning. "You cannot want the dreary wilderness of misery this union will be any more than I do."

"Dreary wilderness?" A tendon flexed in his cheek.

"Yes. Whatever effect the romantic memories you have of me are having on you are transient. I will soon become familiar to your eye. This is a marriage of inconvenience not convenience. Can't you see and I...oh—"

Two darkly dressed seedy men had stolen from behind the thick tree trunk and rushed toward them. Closing the gap within a few fast paces.

"Frank!" She gasped as the glint of a knife flashed before her, and she was dragged to the right in a tight grip.

At the same time, a cruel-looking bone-handled dagger was slashed through the air in front of Frank's face.

He stepped backward, shock flashing in his eyes.

"Hand over your coins and watch." The first of the two tall men snarled at Frank. He had a black scarf tied around the lower half of his face, and he wielded the lethal dagger like a sword.

Anna wriggled, fear filling her as well as the instinct to run. They were being robbed in broad daylight. Robbed...or worse.

"Hand over, or she gets it," the man at Anna's side growled.

Suddenly a knife was jabbing into her waist, not hard, but the point of it easily felt through the material of her gown.

"Frank!" She froze, gripped by terror. One shove and it would all be over for her.

"Please, don't hurt her," Frank said. "You can have everything I have on me."

"Hurry." The other dagger was swiped Frank's way again.

"Yes, here. But don't hurt my wife." Frank withdrew his fob watch, snapping it from the pocket. "Take this." He set his attention on Anna. "And I have coins, too, but if you hurt her, you won't get any of it."

"Give me the coins." The man at his side snatched the watch and shoved it in his pocket.

"Please, let us go," Anna said, her voice shaking and her throat tight.

"Shut it," the man at her side growled. "You're swimming in lard, and we have naught a feather to fly with."

"I have four coins." Frank flashed the coins in his palm, a blue ribbon sat with them, also tugged from his pocket. He curled his fingers into a fist. "You can have them when you remove that knife from my wife's side and step away from her."

"We're in charge. Don't forget that." The man with the dagger lunged at Frank.

Frank swiftly side stepped, ducking beneath a branch and putting distance between himself and the first man's dagger. "No. I am in charge. And I will give you what I have on me this day in order for you to leave, and nothing will be spoken of this again. But if you harm one hair on my bride's head, I will use everything in my considerable power to hunt you down and see that you are hanged from this very tree with a crowd to watch your last breath."

The man with the dagger glanced at his accomplice. After a moment, he said, "Leave her be. Step away."

"No. He ain't handed over the money."

"I will," Frank said. "As soon as you move away from the lady. What's more, I will not give chase or summon help."

"Don't believe him," the man holding Anna snapped. His breath was foul despite him also having a scarf around his face. "A beau like him thinks of nothing but his bloody self."

Anna's knees were trembling. All she could feel was the knife pressing into her side. All she could see was the ugly dagger being waved Frank's way.

What if Frank pushed these violent, greedy men too far with his words and demands, and they both took a stabbing? What if he got struck in the heart? Died? Bled out beneath this oak tree. How would she ever be able to live? Surely her heart would stop, break, fall apart with sadness.

"Damn it." The man holding her huffed.

Suddenly she was shoved to the right. She stumbled, and her foot caught in her gown. Slamming to the ground, her knees hit a root, and her palms rough, dry earth. She cried out and spun to face Frank.

He threw the coins into the light of the day. The ribbon fluttered into the air, then billowed to the grass. "Take them and rot in Hell."

The two men rushed after the money, pocketing it in seconds and taking off.

And then Frank was next to her, on his knees, examining her side where the knife had been pressed. "Anna. Anna. Are you hurt?"

"No. No. I don't think so." Her heart was beating wildly. She wondered if she might be sick. "Are…are you?"

"Am I what?" He gripped her shoulders and studied her face.

"Hurt? Are you hurt, Frank? Stabbed?"

He frowned. "It is you I am concerned about." A shard of anguish sliced over his eyes. "Did that brute draw blood? Did he pain you in any way? You are white as a sheet. I fear you are bleeding"

"No." She shook her head and glanced down at her gown. "Perhaps a stitch will be needed in the material but not in my flesh."

"Thank the heavens for that." He touched the tiny hole in her gown, then cupped her cheeks in both of his palms. "For I would never have forgiven myself if anything had happened to you at the hands of those thugs."

"Frank." She stared into his eyes and saw the Frank she used to know. The one she'd loved. The one who'd loved her. The years and everything that had come between them faded away. As if coming close to losing each other through death had not only shrunk but erased the misdeeds they'd committed against each other.

"A husband's duty is to protect his wife," Frank said softly, "to care for her, ensure no harm befalls her. I intend to carry out my duty as your husband, today and forever."

They were both on their knees. She clung to the lapels of his coat so hard her knuckles paled. "I knew you would defend me." She paused. "Even at the expense of yourself."

"I would give my life for you…" He drew his face closer to hers. "Because you have been the most important person in the world to me since the day I met you. Even when we were not together for all of that time. It is you, Anna, you that I love with all of my heart, and I could not live without you. I do not wish to live without you."

Her eyes filled with hot tears.

"And I meant what I said," he went on. "My vengeance would have had no bounds had they hurt you. My threats to see them hanged were not empty words."

"I know." And she did. She could feel the sincerity coming off him in waves. And in that moment, she knew they could move forward. The past was in the past. Fate or destiny or the Black Widow had given them a second chance, and she was going to grab hold of her future, a future with Frank Webb, Viscount De-Wold.

CHAPTER TWELVE

FRANK STARED AT his beautiful wife, his heart thudding with the reaction to run or fight. Life or death.

He'd been prepared to do either. What he wasn't prepared to do was see his wife held hostage, threatened and terrified. Heaven forbid, hurt.

Now, beneath the oak tree, holding her face, she felt so delicate, so fragile. Her skin was almost translucent and her pretty eyes, wide. He felt like his heart would burst with love and protectiveness. He only ever wanted to see her smiling and happy. He'd make sure this never happened again.

He glanced around, ensuring their assailants had gone. They had. They were alone. The other park goers were in the distance, which was likely why they'd been singled out and attacked.

"Frank," she said, a single tear escaping her right eye and rolling down her cheek. "I am sorry."

"For what?"

"For everything. For not reading your letter, for being so cold on our wedding day, for—"

"Shh, I do not wish for your apologies."

"But—"

"I just wish for you to be well. For you to be my Anna again."

Another tear escaped, and he caught both with the pads of his thumbs and brushed them aside.

"I will always be your Anna."

Her words tightened his own throat, making it feel stuffed with wool and his lower eyelids prickled. "Do you promise?"

"Yes. The good Lord just showed us how abominable it would be to be parted again, this time by death, yet we were shown mercy. We have to learn from that lesson."

"And give thanks to have found each other once more."

"Yes. I give thanks for that." A fresh set of tears escaped.

Frank could hold off no longer. Not another second. He brought her face close and pressed his lips to hers, tasting the salt of emotion as their mouths connected.

It was like coming home, kissing Anna. She'd been in all of his fantasies. The woman he'd longed to find again, and now she was here, and she was his, and there was no damn way he was letting her slip through his fingers.

The kiss deepened. She moaned softly and pressed up against him.

His body reacted, heating, hardening. He could think of nothing but her. It was as if she consumed him and owned his soul.

"My love," he murmured against her lips. "I don't know how I even managed to breathe without you in my life."

"I feel like I can finally breathe again." She giggled. "Except I'm feeling a little breathless right now."

"We should get back to the house." He took her hands and helped her to stand. "Are you sure you're unharmed?"

She examined her palms, several specks of dirt and grit had dented her flesh.

Gently he brushed it away. "I should hunt those monsters down." Anger swarmed again.

"No. It's over now, and we have lived to tell the tale." She touched his cheek. "Let us put it behind us."

He took a deep breath. Easier said than done, but he said it anyway. "I will do as you bid, *mon ange.*"

Her mouth parted, and she stared up at him, pupils wide.

"I cannot call you that anymore?"

"Yes, I…it is just so long since I have heard you say it."

"You should get used to hearing it often. Because you are my angel, always have been and always will be."

He stepped to the left and retrieved the ribbon.

"What is that?" she asked.

"Don't you remember?" He held it out, the ends were frayed.

She shook her head.

"It is yours." He paused. "That day in the stable. I took it from your hair."

She gasped. "Yes. You did. And you…?"

"Kept it? Carry it with me everywhere? Yes, both of those things." He pocketed it again. "It was all I had of you."

"You have all of me now."

Smiling, he held out the crook of his arm. "Now let us get out of this park. I have had quite enough of it for one day, and I have other plans…as I have all of you now."

She slipped her hand into the crook of his elbow. "Other plans?"

"Yes. Something I have been planning on doing since I was a youth blinded by love and heated by desire."

"Frank?"

He tipped his head closer to hers. "You know what I am talking about. Do not pretend that you don't."

"I do know." A rise of color returned to her chalk-white cheeks. "But it is daylight, and the staff and—"

"The staff will not disturb us, and as for it being daylight. We are man and wife, so that matters not." He paused and curled his hand over hers. "And did it matter in the stable that time? I don't think it did, not a jot. We would have taken what we'd both needed if left undisturbed with no care for the time of day."

She stared straight ahead as they rejoined the path.

"And I do not mean that I would have taken your virginity," he went on. "You'd made it clear that was to remain intact. But I would have found other ways to have you panting with pleasure, calling out my name in ecstasy. Squirming and squealing in bliss."

"Lord above!" She glanced around. "You cannot say such crude things in the park. Someone might hear."

"I want *you* to hear."

"Well…I…you just shouldn't, it's not proper."

"And who is to stop me?" He grinned. "And besides, I only speak the truth."

"I know not what you speak of." She tilted her chin. "As you well know."

"All the more reason for us to hurry, so I can show you what you missed out on that day."

"It was a long time ago."

"But your sweet body still remembers, still yearns for the satisfaction only I can give you."

She said nothing as they walked through the park gate to the street.

He drew her hand to his lips and kissed her knuckles. "How lucky I am to have you as my bride."

And lucky was exactly how he felt. He could barely contain the happiness coursing through him. It was like golden syrup and fine wine and spiced fruit all combined. And the ache in his lower abdomen, his groin—for the first time ever he believed he was going to be able to truly satisfy his needs.

But not until he'd taken care of all of Anna's needs. She was his number one priority.

THEY ARRIVED AT the townhouse, and Frank led Anna up the stone steps.

Her heart was thudding, a combination of the fright they'd had, the relief of admitting her feelings for Frank, and having those emotions returned—and the now very real prospect of laying with a man...Frank...for the first time.

The polished black door was pulled open the moment they reached it.

"My lord." Bannister nodded at Anna. "My lady."

Frank nodded at him and drew her inside.

"Shall I prepare tea in the drawing room?" Bannister asked, reaching for Frank's jacket and helping him shrug out of it.

"No, thank you." Frank's movements were hasty as he tugged Anna's light shawl from around her shoulders and thrust it into Bannister's arms atop his jacket.

Bannister appeared slightly shocked at the swift action. "Perhaps you are hungry. Shall I have Cook prepare a selection of sandwiches and pastries?"

"Absolutely not." Frank weaved his fingers with Anna's.

She clutched his hand; her palms were hot.

"I'm sorry." Bannister paused. "Lemonade in the courtyard perhaps?"

"We wish for only one thing you can give us," Frank said, urging Anna toward the staircase. "And that is to be undisturbed."

"I beg your pardon."

"I trust the housemaid has finished her duties in our bedchambers?"

"I believe so, my lord."

"Good." Frank took the first few stairs at a hasty pace. "Then I must insist that you leave us be. My wife and I have plans for the afternoon. The entire afternoon."

"Frank." A prickle of embarrassment went up Anna's spine and over her scalp. The way Frank was half dragging her up the stairs with undisguised earnestness would make it quite clear to Bannister exactly what those plans were.

"Do not worry yourself." Frank released her hand and slipped his arm around her waist, drawing her close as they neared the top of the staircase. "For no man on God's earth would blame me for being eager to consummate this marriage. You are beautiful and intelligent and a woman who knows her own mind. Surely that is what every fellow desires."

"Well, I—"

"And you are mine. Today, tomorrow, forever." He led her along the landing and paused outside what she presumed was his bedchamber, as it was the door alongside hers. He cupped her cheek and stared into her eyes. "And I intend to claim you as such. As mine. For all of time."

His gaze was penetrating and firm, and a rush of desire flooded her system. Her knees weakened, and heat pooled in her belly and lower, between her legs.

"I will be the only man to ever lay in your bed," he said, his voice low and husky. His thumbs stroked her cheek. "The only man to ever touch you, bring you pleasure, and as such, I promise you the same in return." He paused. "And I hope that you will give me a son and heir."

"I want that, too, Frank. All of it."

Suddenly he released her and pushed open the door.

The room was in semi darkness owing to the heavily swagged blue and gold drapes at the window, and a fire was stacked ready to be lit. The four-poster bed had coverlets that matched the curtains, and a vase of lilac flowers sat on a table beside a wingback chair.

But that was all that Anna managed to see because then the door slammed shut and Frank swept her into his arms. His mouth caught hers in a hungry kiss, stealing her breath away.

For a moment, she was back in the stable at the De-Wold estate. Diamond watching on as Frank touched her hair, built up the tension in her body, then set about releasing it.

Only this time, they wouldn't be disturbed. This time he would take it all the way.

There was no reason for him not to.

"Frank," she managed as he sent his kisses over her cheek and to the curve of her neck. His hands were on her behind, palming each buttock.

"Yes, *mon ange?*"

"I..." She didn't know how to say it. She had no idea what to do. How this worked. She knew she liked his touch and his kisses, but what more should she do?

"Do not fear." He reached for the gown's buttons that ran from her nape to the hollow of her back. "I will not hurt you."

"It is not that." She studied his face. "I just don't know what to do, and I want it to be good for you, too."

He grinned, his dimple digging probably the deepest she'd ever seen it. "That is what you are concerned about?"

"Yes. I do not want to disappoint you."

"You are alone in this room with me, as my wife, and you are willing, are you not?"

"Yes. Of course, but—"

"There is no but. You have already made me the happiest man in England just by being here." He paused as he undid the last button. "There is no room for disappointment, I assure you."

Her dress loosened, threatening to slip down and expose her breasts and undergarments.

"So just relax," he said, his voice softer now. "Trust me, and I'll ensure we both get what we need."

As he'd spoken, he'd gently tugged at her dress, encouraging it to fall to her waist, then lower still, until it pooled at her feet.

Instinct sent her arms over her chest, covering her breasts and hard, tight nipples.

"No." He gently took her wrists. "Let me look at you, it has been my greatest wish for as long as I can remember to see you this way."

She swallowed, her throat tight as he removed her arms from their modest position and allowed his gaze to roam her breasts. It was as if he were drinking her in with his eyes. He licked his lower lip and pulled in a deep breath. "You are so beautiful."

"I am yours."

"My new favorite three words." He cupped her right breast and stepped in closer.

And then he was kissing her, squeezing and releasing her soft flesh as his tongue probed her mouth.

She wrapped her arms over his shoulders but was instantly frustrated by the amount of material there. She wanted to touch his skin, learn his shape, too.

After fumbling with his cravat, she managed to free it and allowed it to drop to the floor. She swiftly undid his waistcoat buttons, and as he stooped to take her right nipple into his mouth, she discarded that.

"Oh, Frank." She slotted her hands into his thick hair and arched her back. The wet warmth of his mouth was bliss, and her nipple hardened further. A white-hot zing of pleasure shot between her legs, creating a throbbing need.

A need she'd always had to fulfill herself in the past.

But that had all changed now.

"You taste like honey," he said, moving to her left nipple. "The sweetest thing I have ever experienced."

She clutched at his shirt, fearing she might fall over. What he was doing was so intense and exactly what she needed.

"Steady," he said, circling her waist and rising up. "We have barely started, and I can't have you fainting on me."

"I'm not going to faint." Her hands were shaking as she dragged his shirt from his waistband. "Because that would extend the wait for what is to happen, and it has been too many years as it is."

"I couldn't have said it better myself." He raised his hand over his head and fisted his shirt between his shoulder blades. And then he was dragging it over his head. Messing his hair further as the shirt was abandoned.

They came together in a frantic kiss. Chests pressing in tight, hearts thudding as one.

The bedding was soft and cool on her back and an erotic shiver danced over her skin.

"You are cold?" he asked against her lips.

"No. I am hot."

"Good." He kissed the hollow of her throat, then licked down her chest.

She moaned and fisted the sheets. His mouth was leaving a trail of needy pleasure.

Once again, he laved at her nipples, each in turn, and as he did so, his hand was busy discarding her gown and petticoat, which fell from the bed along with her shoes.

Drawing up her legs, her white-stockinged knees grazed his hips, and she felt for a moment what it would be like to have him there, his size, his weight, his heat.

"Frank," she moaned. "Oh…please."

"I know what you need." He sat back on his haunches and curled his fingers into the waistband of her drawers. "And to give it to you, these must go."

She didn't argue, instead she wriggled and maneuvered until the drawers were gone, and all that remained were the stockings.

"My love," he murmured, running his hand from her right ankle to her thigh and then to the patch of hair that sat at the junction of her legs. "You are more lovely than I could ever have imagined.

She resisted the urge to snap her legs closed. Not that she could have very easily because he was kneeling between them.

"I have kissed your mouth, your breasts," he said, stroking over her most intimate folds. "And now I will kiss you here."

He was going to do what?

"Relax and enjoy," he said. "And think only of pleasure."

Before she could say anything, he'd buried his face between her legs and slid one long finger into her cunny. "Oh!"

Once again, she speared her fingers into his hair. Her belly trembled as she looked downward. His nose was buried in her tuft, and she didn't need to be able to see his tongue to know he was stroking firm circles over her small nub of need.

"Frank. Oh…I didn't…expect…know…oh…" She dropped her head back. Did all married couples do this? She had no idea. But she was glad they were. Frank was getting it just right, feeding all the hot damp places between her legs that needed nourishing.

Within minutes, the pressure built. He added another finger into her cunny, and she hugged it with her internal muscles and thrashed her head from left to right. "Oh…it feels so good. Don't stop."

She'd never have believed she'd say such demanding words. Be so wanton. But her body's desires had taken over. She needed release, and she needed it fast.

CHAPTER THIRTEEN

FRANK REVELED IN the musky scent and taste of Anna, the hot grip of her cunny around his fingers and the sweet sounds of pleasure as he worked her.

His cock was so hard, he feared it might burst free of his breeches. His balls were tight and his belly a riot of excitement and need. He'd lost count of the number of times he'd dreamed of having her spread before him like this, and he thanked his lucky stars he'd had a good teacher in Paris. He was getting it just right. Not just by the gasps and groans filling the bedchamber but also the heated dampness leaking from her onto his hand and chin.

She was getting close. Her body readying itself for his cock. He'd have to play it careful because he wanted to be inside her, properly inside her, when she hit her climax.

"Oh, Frank. I'm going to…it's so good…oh how did you know that doing that would…ohh…"

He lifted up, grabbling with his breeches to release his cock. Irritated when his fingers caught in the material.

"Frank," she wailed. "Oh, but…"

"I told you to trust me, I know what you need," he said, gripping his solid erection and pulling it free. "Exactly what you need."

Her line of sight dipped low, to his cock, and her eyes widened. "Oh, dear Lord."

"Relax," he said, lining up the tip with her entrance. "This is what we've waited so long for."

She grasped his biceps, her fingers digging into his flesh. "I thought it once before, in the kitchen garden, but now I am sure, that will never fit, not in there."

"It will. We were made for each other." He was hot, perspiration dotting his forehead. "Try and let me in." He touched the end of his cock to her inviting, wet entrance.

Her eyes were wide, and she bit on her bottom lip.

"Relax," he said. "And soon you will be reaching that point of bliss with me inside you." He managed a tight smile. "It will be amazing. For both of us."

She didn't answer, so he eased in just an inch. The urge to forge deep, in the space of one heartbeat, was almost overwhelming, but he kept a hold of his control—even though he only gripped it by the last thread.

"Oh, yeah," he said, locking his elbows and watching his cock disappear. "That's it, oh damn that's good."

She drew her legs up, clamping her stockinged knees to his hips, and it almost tipped him over the edge. Anna was his every fantasy come true. He'd never been with a woman like her. And she was his. He'd never let her go.

"Frank." She cupped his cheek and drew his attention to her face. "I...oh..."

"You're doing it. You're taking me." He kept on going, slowly, almost painfully slow. Feeling each tiny section of her smooth cunny grasping his cock in wet heat. Soon he felt his balls press up against her, and his cock could sink no more.

"You've done it," he said, dipping to kiss her. "My cock is in you, deep, so deep."

"I know," her voice was tight. "And oh my, it's…"

"It's going to start getting even better, right now." He dropped his weight so his body came into contact with her swollen, needy bud.

The moment he that did, she gasped and her eyes widened.

"Now you will know what it is like to find true pleasure," he said, riding over her so he stimulated the exact spot she craved pressure.

She grasped a fistful of his hair and tugged. "Oh!"

"You like that?" he asked.

She nodded, her breaths coming fast and shallow.

"You want more?" He rubbed over her again, a luxurious long ride.

Her cunny fluttered and constricted, and she bucked up to meet him. "Yes. Oh…please."

"Take what you need," he said, hoping his seed wouldn't spurt from him until she'd climaxed. "Take what you need beautiful bride of mine."

Setting up a steady, firm rhythm, he rode over her, sinking deep each time. He wanted to kiss her, but that would mean missing the expression of desperate bliss washing over her face. She was staring up at him with such intensity, he was sure she could see into his soul.

"Can you find your satisfaction?" he managed after a few minutes.

"Yes…can you?"

"The very moment…you do." And he hoped that would be soon. Stamina had never been an issue before, but Anna was like no other. His *mon ange* had him on the edge of control.

Sliding her hands down his hot back, she shoved at his breeches, then grasped his buttocks, one in each palm.

"Anna," he gasped, his cock swelling further. Her small, hot hands on him was heavenly.

"Don't stop." She pressed her head onto the pillow, arched her neck, and closed her eyes. For a moment, she held her breath, her lips a tight stern line, and then she cried out, a strangled sound at first that drew to a moan of pure bliss.

Frank gave up the fight. As her cunny pulsated around his cock, he released his seed. The pleasure of it rushing up his shaft had him also crying out, the sound mixing with her ecstasy.

He half withdrew, then blasted in again, pushing the air from her lungs and struggling to catch his own breath. The relief was exquisite. It flowed from him and washed over his skin, trembling up his spine and flashing bright lights over his eyes.

Never had he felt such extreme pleasure, such pure relief at being able to spill his desire.

"Frank!"

She cried out his name, and he dropped over her, kissing her, winding his arms beneath her and holding her as close as he could get her. Their bodies were as one. Sweat slicked their flesh together. She wrapped her legs around the backs of his, and he kissed her so deeply, he barely knew where he stopped and she began.

Eventually her cunny relaxed and his cock relaxed.

"How did that feel?" he whispered against her lips.

"How do you think it felt?"

He felt her smile. "It sounded like I got it just right, *mon ange.*"

"You are not in the least befogged by how that made me feel," she squeezed his behind. "You heard and felt my pleasure."

"You can't blame me for wanting to be sure." He kissed the tip of her nose. "For I intend to bed you every night for the rest of our lives."

"Oh, is that right?" She giggled, still breathless.

"Yes, so it is essential I have the technique perfected."

She giggled again. "I would say it's pretty perfect already, but I can't see the harm in practicing if it is going to feel like that every time."

It was his turn to laugh. "Why, I do believe I have quite the corky little wife."

"Would you have me any other way? Surely it is better to be lively in the bedchamber than a sack of potatoes."

"Sack of potatoes, that you could never be." He rolled over, pulling her with him so he stayed inside her but she was on top of him.

"Frank." She steadied herself with her palms on his chest. "What are you doing?"

"There are many ways to find our pleasure," he said, reaching for a large silver pin that held her hair up at the crown. He pulled it out and tossed it aside.

"There are?"

"Yes." He helped her hair tumble down over her shoulders, finally getting the image he'd dreamed of all these years. "And when my cock hardens again, we will practice another way."

"Which is?" She squirmed a little as though encouraging his next erection.

Blood rushed to his groin again. "You will ride me, Anna, and I will get to see your sweet body atop me as you bring us both to pleasure."

"Oh, but I—"

He pressed his finger to her lips. "There are no buts in pleasure. And no limits between a man and wife. You are all I want, all I have ever wanted." He paused to keep control of his emotions. "Your happiness is mine. I only ever want to see you smile, *mon ange.*"

As THE SUN faded in the sky, striping it with pink, orange and lilac, Frank held a sleeping Anna in his arms.

They'd made love all afternoon, finding and giving pleasure until they were exhausted. He hadn't even cared that the staff might hear them. For he'd finally found the one who'd got away. And what was more, he'd made her his wife.

The new Viscountess De-Wold.

It terrified him that he'd been so close to losing her within hours of getting her back. He'd never forget the sight of the knife at her side, the whiteness of her skin, the terror that ran like acid through his veins as he battled to keep his cool and get them out of the hideous, volatile situation.

It wasn't a situation he intended to encounter again, and there was only one way to make sure that didn't happen. For now, at least.

"Mmm, I'm thirsty," Anna said sleepily.

"I will ring for high tea." He kissed her forehead, then stood naked from the bed. He took a moment to lock his fingers and stretch his arms over his head, easing out the muscles he'd been working hard. He yawned.

"Husband, I do believe you are still tired even though you have slept this last hour."

"Tired but happy." He grinned and pulled the lever to summon Bannister. "How could I not be with you in my bed?" He studied her mussed up hair spread on the pillow. The flush in her cheeks and her rosy pink nipples peeking from the blankets. Was it possible for a man's heart to burst with love. It felt like it could be.

Knock. Knock.

Anna yanked up the blanket as Frank hastily pulled on a burgundy silk robe and knotted it at his waist. "Enter."

Bannister appeared. "You called, my lord."

"Yes. We are hungry and thirsty if you could prepare a tray."

"For the drawing room?"

"No. Deliver it here."

He hesitated, as if this was a most unusual request, but then, "As you wish, my lord." He backed out, shutting the door with a click.

Frank grinned. "He'll get used to us spending many hours in the bedchamber."

"But we must do other things." She sat, her hair falling over her breasts and half concealing them.

Frank sat on the side of the bed and took her hand. "Yes. You are quite right, and there is something we will do first thing tomorrow."

"There is?" Her eyebrows raised.

"Yes, we will journey to Staffordshire, to the De-Wold estate."

She was quiet, though he knew the spindles of her mind were working.

"I do not wish for you to walk in the park until the assailants have been apprehended," he said. "It is not safe, and I cannot bear the thought of anything happening to you." He turned her hand over and kissed her palm. "Not when I have only just found you again."

Still, she remained quiet.

"You do not wish to go to the De-Wold estate? It is your new home, Anna."

"It is not that, it is just…"

"Tell me. We must be honest with each other on all matters."

A frown creased her brow. "It is because your mother will be there."

"Yes. She lives there most of the year."

"She will be most put out by our union. We have discussed this already."

"We should give her a chance and—"

"On the day I left the De-Wold estate with my mother, I recall looking from my bedchamber window for the last time." She tilted her chin, her jaw tensing. She glanced out of the window.

He said nothing. He remembered that dreadful day, too. Anna leaving was like having his arms and legs ripped from his body, yet he'd had to smile, take a stroll, take tea, make polite conversation, and then thank his mother for putting such wonderful opportunities before him. All he'd wanted to do was gallop as far away as he could on Diamond. Rush. Race. Find Anna and never let her go.

Anna carried on. "I saw the chaise arrive, drawn by fine two bays. And from it alighted Lady Elizabeth Burghley with her mother. Dressed in a silken lemon gown with matching hat and gloves, she was the epitome of elegance and class. Everything I knew I wasn't. And your mother, she was beaming as you took that gloved hand before offering your arm and taking Lady Elizabeth on a stroll to the lake." She paused, swallowed. "I could hardly see straight for the tears flowing from my eyes, hardly stand straight for the pain in my chest." She pressed her hand to her right breast. "It is something I will never forget. How quickly I was replaced, how lowly I was."

"You were not replaced, that could never happen." He shook his head and squeezed her hand. "Lady Elizabeth was not the one for me, and we knew that very quickly. In fact, she is now married, I believe. I received not a second glance my way from her, and she the same from me."

Anna nodded. "I am glad for her if she is now happily married, truly. But your mother viewed me then as wholly unsuitable as your wife because of my class. That will not have changed. And add to that the way we married in secret, in haste, her fury will be tenfold what I have seen in the past."

"Do not be so harsh on her. Losing Father so suddenly, that was hard, it took its toll."

"You really think she will be pleased when she hears our news? That I am the new Viscountess De-Wold?"

Frank sighed. The truth was his mother was likely to be incredibly miffed. What Anna had said was true, and there was no love lost between the two women. Though that would have to change.

"I think it will take her some time to get used to," he said.

Anna laughed. "It will take more than time."

"You have a point, she will also have to see the truth," he went on, "that you are the new Viscountess De-Wold, the mistress of the house. And as such, final decisions on hiring staff, menus, interior design, and to some extent finances, will fall to you now." He allowed his words to settle. "I believe she will be pleased to have that burden taken from her. It has been hers to shoulder for many years."

"Pleased?" Anna huffed. "I think she will be furious that you have brought her to a *point pon plus*. She has no options, no way to turn."

"That is true, she can hardly annul our marriage now." He leaned forward and kissed her softly. "Thank the good Lord for that."

She managed a small smile. "Perhaps we could wait a few more days."

"You wish to delay facing her?"

"No, it is not that, it's just…"

"We would do better to tell her before she hears it from someone else, don't you think? That would really inflame the situation."

She sighed.

"It is better she hears it from me before she reads any announcement or is told of one. More likely she'll accept our marriage from the start that way."

"I cannot disagree that it would be better she hears it from you, but her accepting our union, I'm afraid I hold no optimism for that being anything other than a very rocky ride."

"My love." He pulled her into his arms. "I do not wish you to worry your pretty head about this a moment longer. I am your husband now, and I will see to this matter. All I ask is you keep your cool, even if she doesn't keep hers."

"I will try, but—"

"But?"

"There is the other matter."

"Which is?"

"I also don't know how I will ever face Cook."

"Because…?"

"Oh Frank, because if you remember, she was there, that day, in the garden when…"

120

"When you touched my cock. The first woman ever to, might I add." He grinned.

She pursed her lips, and a little color stained her cheeks.

"Of course, I remember," he said. "But do not worry about a servant's thoughts."

"But she's full of tittle-tattle, she's bound to cause ructions and spread—"

"She will do no such thing, and if she does, she will be out on her ear, that is your discretion as lady of the house. You can hire and dismiss at will."

"But the thought of sending someone packing…leaving their home and job. I know what that is like."

"Never fear. I will have stern words said to her, and if she dares disobey, I will relieve her of her duties in an instant. You will not have to worry yourself with it." The wave of protectiveness he had for his new wife was becoming familiar whenever he thought of something or someone that might harm or upset her.

"You would do that?"

"Of course." He took both of her hands. "I will do anything for you, and you can rest assured, you will be respected at the De-Wold estate, not just by my mother but by all of the staff."

For a moment she was silent, then, "Can I make one request?"

"You can ask me for the moon and I will set out to get it, *mon ange.*"

"It is not the moon I desire." She paused. "It is my new lady's maid, Mary. She is kind, and I believe her to be loyal of nature. I would like it very much if she accompanied me to Staffordshire."

"That is a small ask. I will see to it that she travels in a second carriage tomorrow."

"Thank you, but are you sure that is not asking too much?"

"Not at all. I have samples of fabric here in London that I wish to take to the factory. A coach was following along anyway. I'm sure

Mary will be quite comfortable. And if it is Mary you wish as your lady's maid, then that is the way it will be."

She let out a small sigh. "Thank you. That makes me feel better."

He smiled and kissed her. "I know how to make you feel much better. Much, much better." He pressed over her, urging her to lie down, then flattening himself over her. Desire spilled into his veins, and the need to feel flesh on flesh became overwhelming.

Knock. Knock.

"Lawds," he muttered. "Supremely bad timing."

She laughed. "Perhaps we should have sustenance if we are to keep up these energetic pursuits."

"Mmm, maybe you're right. But don't think I've forgotten exactly where I was and exactly what I was just about to do."

Chapter Fourteen

T HE NEXT DAY, Anna found herself once again seated in Frank's coach, though this time the journey was much farther than from Whitehall to Mayfair. He'd placed a woollen blanket over her knees with the family crest embroidered into the corner, even though the day was warm.

"I am sorry it has been such a long way, you are likely very weary," he said, reaching for her hand. "It is not far now."

"It is quite agreeable to travel in such style." She gestured around the highly polished interior and the velvety seats decorated with plush cushions. "And with pleasant views, too." She nodded at the window to her right. The gentle hills rolled into the distance, ancient hedgerows blossomed, and the sky held not one cloud.

"Yes. I am always glad to swap the London air for England's greenest hills."

After another thirty minutes, she leaned forward and looked out of the window yet again. Finally, they'd arrived. The De-Wold estate's massive wrought iron gates were open, the two towering stone pillars supporting them topped with lion heads hadn't changed a bit. To the right was the gatekeeper's small, thatched cottage, and he stood outside the black front door and tipped his hat at the coach.

Anna's emotions were at war. For so long she'd wanted to return to this beautiful place, wipe the slate clean, and start again. But now that she was here, she knew, despite her husband's assurances, that it was an impossible ask. Some things couldn't be undone.

"I am excited to have you here." He took her hand. "We will enjoy boating on the lake and swimming. Picnics and nine-pins. We have an even bigger library here for you to enjoy, in fact, it is all yours now, and if you wish to paint or sew, you only have to say the word, and I will ensure you have everything you need."

She looked at his excited face. The way he was speaking, it was as if the obstacle of his mother's disapproval had already been removed. But still Anna smiled. Frank's had always been infectious, and she couldn't help returning it. "Dining *al fresco* with you is certainly something I'd enjoy," she said. "Though swimming. I cannot swim, Frank. When would I have ever learned such a thing?"

"You cannot swim? No, of course, how foolish of me. But never fear." He pointed at the glistening lake through the window. "I will teach you. Within weeks you will be a little fish swimming around the reeds and bulrushes yonder."

She laughed. "I appreciate your confidence, but I don't think so."

"Oh, but you will." He pulled her close and kissed her temple. "A pretty little naked fish dashing through the water. Hair floating behind you like a mermaid and your nipples hard with the chill."

"Frank!" Her cheeks heated just at the thought of being naked in the open with Frank. If the previous afternoon and night were anything to go by, they wouldn't be able to keep their hands off each other. And anyone could come along and see…that was an experience she didn't want to repeat.

He chuckled. "I am glad to be here. My stomach is empty. I long for the peace of the countryside, and I wish to see how Diamond is faring."

The coach crunched over gravel and then came to a halt.

A rush of nerves swarmed over Anna's skin, prickling and tingling and making her gown feel altogether too tight. She pushed the blanket aside.

"Excellent." Frank rubbed his hands together and sat forward on the seat. "Home again."

It was as though he'd completely forgotten the battle with his mother that, without a doubt, lay ahead.

"Ready?" He grinned at her as the door opened.

"I suppose." She gulped as the fresh countryside air flooded the interior, and the sound of evening birdsong filled her ears.

One of the horses snorted, and there was a bang on the back of the coach as luggage was lifted free.

Frank stepped out. "Mother. How lovely to see you."

It was as Anna had expected. A welcome committee awaited.

"Frank. My dearest Frank."

Anna sat on the lip of the seat and peered out.

The Dowager Viscountess, Bertha Webb, embraced her son with her eyes closed as though truly relishing the moment of holding him. He was considerably taller and broader than she, and her head was against his chest.

"How have you been?" Frank asked as they pulled apart.

"It was a most tiresome trip back from London. Florence simply wouldn't settle despite going to the park literally moments before our journey. You know how she hates the carriage. I simply don't know what use she is as a lap dog if she won't sit on my lap."

At that moment, a fluffy white dog shot from the house, down the wide expanse of steps, and began barking at Frank.

"Stop that fuss." Frank bent and tousled the dog's ears.

It stopped barking and wagged its tail wildly as it circled his ankles.

"Mother." Frank straightened. "I have most exciting news."

"You have?" She raised her eyebrows.

"Yes. I have finally taken a wife." He puffed up his chest. "A wife I truly love, always have and always will."

The dowager's mouth fell open, and she pressed her hand to her chest. "I cannot believe these words you speak. After all the years I have spent...after all of the efforts I have gone to match you with someone. And you have found a wife on your own?" She turned to the coach. "And you have her here? With you? Oh, please say you have so I can meet her at once."

"Of course, she is here. I do not wish to be parted from her ever again. Please, alight, Anna, and come and say hello to my mother."

"Anna?" The dowager brushed a stray hair from her cheek. Had she remembered the name after all these years?

Anna took a deep breath and moved into the light of day. A footman held out his hand for her to take as she stepped down to the gravel. Her pale blue gown was creased, and she smoothed it feeling almost unbearably self-conscious.

Bertha pressed her palm to her forehead, a large ruby ring flashing in the evening sun. "But I...it's you!" She peered closer. Eyes narrowing. "I am not wrong. Anna Toussaint. The very same."

"Good day." Anna bobbed her knees and bowed her head.

"Anna Webb." Frank quickly took Anna's hand and tugged her forward. He then wrapped his arm around her waist so her body was flush with his. "Is the new Viscountess De-Wold, and I could not be happier."

Bertha looked as though she could not be more shocked. But she didn't pale; her cheeks reddened. "You! You were banished from this house many years ago. How dare you—"

"Mother." Frank's tone was stern. "I know you've made Anna's acquaintance in the past, but I must insist that as of this very moment, you wipe that from your memory."

"Wipe it from my memory!" She shook her head. "What I saw that day can never be wiped from my memory. And now you dare to bring her here under the pretense that she is your wife." She paused, and her face twisted as if she were in actual physical pain.

"It is no pretense. We are man and wife. The signed register there for all to see. And very soon the announcement will be in the press."

"You must stop the announcement. And undo this madness." She rushed up to Frank and clutched the lapels of his jacket. "I cannot bare the shame, the scandal."

Anna stepped away, her heart thudding. This was even worse than she'd feared.

"It is not a scandal to marry the person who has your heart." Frank frowned down at his mother and took her hands in his. "And I feel no shame of any sort, only happiness. Unimaginable happiness."

"How can you not feel shame? The shame is unbearable. After the tryst you were caught in... with her. Not even promised to each other. And the gossip spread, you know full well it did. It went beyond this household, these walls. Everyone from here to Mayfair knew of this woman's—"

"I have never been one to care for gossip," Frank suddenly bellowed. "And we were both to blame for that little scrape."

His mother appeared momentarily shocked at the volume of his voice but continued nonetheless. "No, my son. You were not to blame. You were young and foolish and bamboozled by a light skirt and—"

"No. I will not have you say such a thing!" Frank held up his hand. "That is preposterous. She is no such thing."

"How do you know?"

"Because I know her, and I thought I knew you, but it is clear you are so high in the instep you care not for my happiness and only what other people think."

She glared at him. "And what of *my* happiness? After losing your father, you have done this to me. How could you? What kind of son are you?"

"I am the kind of son who will not sit back and listen to my wife be insulted. You will accept our marriage, and you will be nothing but civil to Viscountess De-Wold." He held out his arm to Anna. "Come, my dear. I know you are fatigued from our journey. I will order us some tea while we wait for your lady's maid to arrive."

Anna hesitated. It was as if her insides had knotted and someone was yanking them tighter with every exchange between Frank and his mother. This entire thing was a disaster. She was not wanted here and never would be.

"Anna. *Mon ange.*"

"I do not want that woman in my home." Bertha slammed her hands on her hips. "I forbid it."

"You forget, Mother." Frank tugged Anna's hand until it was hooked through the crook of his arm. He curled his fingers over her knuckles, keeping her in place. "I am now the head of this household, which makes me the only person who can forbid anything." He paused and sucked in a breath as though reining in his temper. "And as such, I forbid you—"

"You cannot forbid me anything." For the first time the color did drain from Bertha's cheeks. "I am your mother." She folded her arms tightly over her chest.

"I forbid you," Frank went on ignoring her words, "to be anything other than respectful and civil to the new viscountess. I wish to hear nothing of what went before, and I absolutely will not have her name sullied in any way."

Bertha squashed her lips into a flat line.

"Am I understood?" Frank said calmly.

"You will hear nothing from me because I will take to my bed-chamber until you have come to your senses, son of mine."

"Then you will be there for a very long time, because the truth is, in marrying Anna, I have finally come to my senses and claimed what I have always wanted in my life."

"You cannot be serious."

"I am deadly serious. Anna is my one and only true love. Get used to it." He stepped forward, tugging Anna with him, and they climbed the stone steps, passing Bertha's lady's maid, who stood with her hands clasped and her gaze to the ground.

Anna's heart was beating wildly. She hoped she wouldn't be sick. The encounter couldn't have gone any worse.

"She will never accept me as your wife," she said as they entered the cool-ness of the vast entrance hallway.

"Then her bedchamber walls will be the last that she sees."

"You cannot do that to your mother. I know your heart, Frank. It will not allow it, not when you have calmed and think about it rationally."

"She has made the decision, not me. Perhaps when she has calmed, she will regret her hasty words and a truce will be found." He stopped and slipped his arms around her waist, pulled her close. "But it is you I care about the most, Anna. I want you to be happy in your new home."

"I wish to be happy, too, but not at the expense of your mother."

He brushed his lips over hers. "And this is one of the reasons I love you so much."

"Why?"

"Your sweet and caring nature. My mother has done you wrong, yet still you worry about her wellbeing."

"It is natural to care about the wellbeing of others."

"Natural to you perhaps, but not to everyone." He tucked a strand of hair behind her ear. "Come, we will go to the drawing room and take tea. When your lady's maid arrives, you can rest then bathe before dinner.

ANNA WAS HAPPY to see Mary fussing around in her bedchamber putting away her clothes.

"My lady." Mary bobbed. "I trust you had a good journey."

"Tiring, but at least the weather was pleasant."

"Indeed, it was." Mary returned to the chest. "We made rather a swift departure from London, my lady, but still I managed to get some new dresses and undergarments sent over for you to peruse. A few hats and gloves, too."

"You did?"

"Yes, with the arrangement that any you do not like or do not fit will be returned for a full reimbursement."

"That is incredibly good of you and so thoughtful."

"It is my job to be thoughtful for you, my lady."

"And it is very much appreciated." She lifted a pale pink chiffon gown from the chest. It was dotted with tiny red roses complete with thin stalks and small leaves. The sleeves were puffed with red ribbons on the shoulders. "This is exquisite."

"Isn't it." Mary paused and smiled. "And look, there's an accompanying bandeau that will look so pretty in your hair." She plucked up a strip of stiffened fabric covered in tiny red roses.

"Oh yes, that is so pretty." Anna touched her hair; it was already coming loose from the plait she'd done that morning.

"I will do it for you. I have been told in the past I am very good with dressing ladies' hair."

"You will? You are? I mean, thank you very much."

Mary smiled. "But bathe first, I am sure you wish to remove the dust of the road from your body."

"Yes, that would be most agreeable."

"The tub has been drawn in your bathing room next door."

Anna glanced around. She'd never been in this room before. "The door to the left of the windows. The one to the right leads to his lordship's bedchamber."

"Thank you, oh and Mary."

"Yes, my lady."

"Going forward, can we avoid the jasmine soap? Anything perfumed with jasmine actually."

"Of course, my lady, whatever you wish."

Chapter Fifteen

Four weeks later…

F RANK COULD NOT deny that his mother's stubbornness was both annoying and surprising.

She had left her bedchamber only once since Anna's arrival, and that was to inspect the icehouse, which was reducing prematurely in the ongoing heat of summer. She took all of her meals alone, entertained herself and spoke, in the majority, only to her lady's maid.

Frank had visited her numerous times, each imploring with her to accept his marriage. He'd tried reasoning and demanding, but none of his tactics had got him anywhere.

Right now, he stood in his largest mill. So vast the local population relied upon it almost in their entirety for income. Luckily, it seemed the thirst for cotton, not just in England but worldwide, showed no sign of being sated. And with his new idea of producing velvet alongside cotton weaves, he was sure his father's substantial business would continue for many decades—hopefully he'd pass on an even greater empire to his heir.

An heir. He'd sent a prayer to God in the estate's private chapel that he and Anna be blessed with children, for it would make his life complete.

"My lord, I think you will be very happy with the new textiles," Henry, his chief supervisor, said as he rolled out a section of cloth on a long wooden office table.

"These are replicated from the samples I brought?"

"Yes, my lord."

Frank ran his hand over the soft blue material, examining the loops and the weave. "It is as I had expected."

"I agree. The laborers have worked very hard on it."

Frank peered closer. "Actually, it is even better than the sample. The skill will be noticed by traders that is for sure. We will get a fine price for this."

"I am pleased you are happy."

"More than happy." Frank straightened and clasped Henry's shoulder. "I know I asked a lot of you and the mill to get this reproduced and the first reams running through the looms in such a short space of time and for that I would like to reward everyone."

"You would?" Henry's eyebrows raised. "You will?"

Frank laughed. "Yes. You may have heard I have recently married and that has put me in a most excellent frame of mind, and I wish to share my good fortune in life."

"Congratulations, my lord." Henry dipped his head.

"Which means I would like an extra tuppence given to every worker in their wage packet this week."

"That is very generous, my lord."

"I wish for my laborers to know that I appreciate them, for without workers, I would not have a mill."

"That is very true, my lord, but without you, they would not have jobs and therefore not have food on the table."

"So, we make a jolly good crew." Frank grinned. "Now I must make haste. I will return in a few days, my good fellow, to see how the cotton delivery from the West Indies is faring up."

If anything, the air felt hotter than when Frank had left his estate that morn, the late afternoon reaching sizzling temperatures. It was no wonder there was an issue with the ice house.

He alighted his carriage and was pleased to see his groomsman riding Diamond toward the stables. "Hey," he called. "Wait up."

He strolled over the grass. "How was he today?" He patted Diamond's sweating neck.

"It's hot, my lord, so we took it slow, but he needed some exercise other than…you know…covering mares."

Frank laughed. "I agree. He's in great shape, you've been doing a remarkable job with him while I've been away."

"He has his moments, as all stallions do, but generally he's compliant."

"I always found him as such." Frank paused. "I will ride him out tomorrow, after luncheon, if you could see that he is prepared. Oh, and saddle up one of the more docile horses. I would like my wife to also ride."

"As you wish, my lord." He nodded. "Very good, my lord."

Frank watched as Diamond was ridden away. He still struck a fine shape, his flanks muscular and his neck curved. It was no wonder his stock was of such value.

With a smile, Frank turned to the house. He had plans with his wife, but they weren't likely to be what she was expecting.

ANNA HEARD HER husband's footsteps before she saw him.

Looking up from her seat beside the window in the drawing room, she smiled. "I trust you had a good visit to the mill."

"Particularly good." He grinned and strode over to her. "But I am glad to be home with you." He set his hands on the arms of her chair and leaned forward to kiss her.

"That is a nice greeting." She smiled up at him.

"I missed you."

"You have only been gone a few hours."

"A few hours away from my beautiful wife is a few hours too many." He took hold of her embroidery and set it aside. "Come, let us walk."

"In this heat? Even the birds have taken a rest from singing." She pointed out of the window at a large oak tree that was usually alive with sparrows.

He laughed. "Yes, we will walk even in this heat. Come. You will be glad you did." He took her hands and pulled her to standing.

"I am not convinced of this plan, but I will trust you." She paused. "Are we going to the stables?"

"No." He pressed his lips to her forehead in a lingering kiss. "Not today. I have another plan."

She allowed him to lead her from the drawing room and then paused as Mary helped her on with a sun hat that held a bow at the base of her neck.

"Ah good. Cook has done as I asked." Frank nodded to two large wicker baskets.

"Would you like me to get one of the footmen to carry these for you, my lord?" Mary asked.

"Yes. Good idea." He picked up a sleek bamboo cane with a gold handle and twirled it. "Come, my love, we have a way to go."

"I am becoming more intrigued by this venture," Anna said. "Particularly because you seem so eager."

He laughed. "Eager…yes." He held out his elbow to her.

Anna blinked several times as they stepped out into the bright sunlight. The glare seemed to bounce off every surface, the gravel, the glossy leaves, and the lake in the distance.

The lake.

"Ah," she said as Frank headed in the direction of the large expanse of water. "I think I know what you have in mind."

"You do?"

"Yes, *al fresco* dining beside the lake."

"Indeed, you have made an excellent assumption."

They strode on, Frank relaying all that had happened at the mill that day for he knew Anna was interested in new fabrics.

"And tomorrow," he said as they came to the edge of the lake, the rushes whispering in the light breeze, "we will enjoy some time in the saddle."

"I cannot ride." She laughed.

He leaned close and whispered in her ear. "I beg to differ."

"Frank!" She nudged him and glanced over her shoulder at the footman. "Shh."

He laughed and came to a halt. "Here will do." He indicated a patch of grass that sat before a gap in the reeds. The shallower water lapped against a small shelf of pebbles, and two ducks spotted them and drifted away.

The footman laid out two tartan blankets, one beside the other, and added two plump cushions to the arrangement. He then opened the picnic baskets and began setting out food and drink on a red-checkered cloth. "Would you like me to pour the wine, my lord?"

"Yes, go ahead." Frank sat and set his cane at his side. "This is one of my favorite spots."

"It is beautiful." Anna gathered her skirt and sat next to him. It was strange to be seated on the ground outside, but she didn't mind. From here, she had a wonderful view of the De-Wold house. The first moment she'd seen it she'd loved its grandeur, from the majestic pillars at the front door to the expanse of chimney pots.

She studied the windows, knowing now what lay behind them. To the far right was a set of windows belonging to Bertha's bedchamber. Was she looking out right now? Watching them? Had her mood mellowed? Had her hate abated in any way?

Anna sighed.

"What is it, *mon ange?*" Frank passed her a glass of wine. "You do not like this entertainment I have planned?"

"Yes, yes, of course, I do. Everything is perfect…almost."

"Almost?" He looked up at the footman. "That will be all, thank you. You can leave us now."

"Very good, my lord." He stepped backward a few feet, then turned and walked away.

"Anna. I really do want to make everything perfect for you."

"But how can it be with your mother so angry? I can almost feel her anger coming through the walls of the house, filling the air with distaste at our union."

"She will come around."

Anna laughed, but it held no humor. "Do you really think so?"

"Yes. I do."

"I wish I had your certainty."

"I know her well. She is hot headed and cares far too much about what other people think."

"I care about what she thinks."

"I know you do." He took her hand and kissed her knuckles, beside the ruby ring that had been passed down through generations of his ancestors. "But give it time, and do not let it spoil this, the last of our honeymoon."

"Yes, you are right. I will try to push it from my mind, for this afternoon at least." She sipped her wine. "This is very delicious."

"It is from France, I brought it back with me, but we should enjoy it while we have it, French goods are becoming harder to come by with the war."

"I will be glad when that is over, too."

"I'm sure it will be, though it is not something for a viscountess to worry about."

"Is that right?"

"Yes." He set down his wine and undid the buttons on his tailed jacket. "And I can wait no longer."

"For what?"

"A dip in the lake." He shrugged off his jacket and set it beside the basket. Beside it he added his neck cloth.

"A dip in the lake. So that is why you wanted to picnic here?"

"Yes, come on, won't you join me?" He shrugged his suspenders loose so they hung at his waist.

"I do not have the correct attire." She shook her head. "You go ahead and enjoy yourself."

"Oh no, *mon ange*, you are not getting out of it that easily. All that is needed is a chemise, and I trust you are wearing something of the sort?"

"What kind of question is that even for a husband to ask?" She feigned a shocked expression.

"A practical one." He pulled his shirt over his head, the muscles on his back and shoulders bunching and flexing as he twisted to lay the garment beside his jacket.

A little tremble of interest caught in Anna's stomach, the way it always did when she saw her husband's delectable body being unclothed.

He pushed at his boots and socks, then stood with his hands on his hips. He had a smattering of dark hair in the center of his chest, and the skin around it glistened slightly with perspiration. "Come, wife of mine, swim with me and let us cool down on this hot day."

"You'll recall I cannot swim."

"I plan to teach you." He slipped his buckskin breeches down and kicked them away so he was standing in nothing but white drawers.

"I'm sure it is most uncivilized to be standing there like that."

"Maybe I like being uncivilized." He laughed and tugged her bonnet off. "And I wish you to be, too."

"No, I really don't."

"It is not a request, Anna." He pulled her to standing. "Now you can either remove your gown yourself or have me do it." He reached for the bow that held the neckline secure. "Which is it to be?"

She laughed and batted his hand away. "You win, you win, but let me do it myself, you tore the stitching on the last gown you decided needed to be hastily removed."

"Ah yes, I am sorry about that." He didn't look sorry in the slightest as he reached for his glass of wine, then stood tall and drank it down in one go. "Ah that is better." He tossed it to the picnic blanket. "You have one minute and then I am coming to get you."

And with that, he turned and waded into the shallows, within seconds he was up to his thighs and then lunged forward, diving beneath the dark surface.

"Frank!" Anna stepped forward, fearful that he'd disappeared from view.

But within seconds, he'd surfaced nearer the middle of the lake, flicking his head to get his hair from his eyes. "It's wonderfully refreshing."

"I'm sure it is." She toed off her pumps, then slipped off her white stockings. She knew one thing for sure about her husband, if he said he wanted her to go in the lake with him, he would get his own way.

With a glance at the house, she pulled up the hem of her gown to reveal her white chemise. Carefully, she slipped it off, glad now that she'd gone without a corset today, not just because of the heat but also because of the fuss to remove it.

With her gown atop Frank's clothing, she stepped down to the water's edge. The breeze pressed her silky chemise against her body, and her nipples hardened. She felt brazen yet free, erotic yet at one with nature.

"Oh, it's cold," she said, dipping her right big toe in.

"It only feels that way because you are so hot." Frank flipped onto his back and rotated his arms, propelling himself toward a patch of bulrushes. A reed warbler sat on one, singing loudly or perhaps warning of the invasion on his territory.

Anna stepped into the water. The pebbles were hard and uneven and shifted beneath her soles, wafting up a cloud of dusky silt that caressed her toes.

"Keep going," he called.

With her arms held out for balance, she took another step, covering her ankles with the gently lapping water. She laughed. "This is as deep as I'm going."

"Oh really." He stopped swimming on his back and flipped to his front.

"Yes, really."

"We'll see about that."

Within a few seconds, he was striding out of the water in front of her. His hair was plastered to his head and drips ran from his nose and chin, falling over his broad chest in rivulets and streams. His drawers clung to his groin, leaving little to imagination, and his strong thigh muscles tensed as he pushed against the water.

Anna didn't think she'd ever seen him more dashing than in that moment. Her heart did a little squeeze of love and longing.

"Anna," he said, grinning. "You can do better than that."

"I don't know if I can, I...oh!"

He'd captured her around the waist, pressing his cool, wet body up against hers. "You can't swim in the shallows."

"I don't want to go deep."

"You won't, I promise." He tugged her forward a few steps. The water quickly came up to her knees. "Besides, I've got you."

"Do you promise?"

"Absolutely."

They went deeper, and she clutched his arm as the cool spread up her thighs and her toes sank into soft sand, or was it mud? "Are there fish in here?"

"No, only eels."

"Eels!" She squealed.

He laughed, a deep guffaw that rippled over the water. "No. I am jesting."

"Well don't." She banged her fist on his hard, wet shoulder. "I do not wish to swim with eels."

"You are only paddling."

"And that will do for today." She turned to him and held onto both of his shoulders, the water was skimming her upper thighs, catching in the gap between them.

"One more step," he said.

"Only one more?"

"Yes, only one more." He urged her a little deeper.

She gasped as wet coolness washed over her cunny. Her chemise floated on the surface.

"How does that feel?" he asked, locking his fingers in the small of her back and holding her close.

"Cold."

"I mean…" He dipped his head so his nose touched hers. "How does it really feel?"

She pulled in a breath. He was hard against her, his cock a solid wedge of flesh trapped between them.

"Unusual," she managed. "Not at all like bathing in warm water."

"The cold makes you feel alive? Yes?"

"Yes."

"And you can feel every part of your body."

"Yes."

He kissed her and slipped his right hand over her buttock to squeeze it gently.

She moaned into his mouth. It was surely scandalous to feel so full of desire when out in the open, but she couldn't help herself. His touch flicked a switch in her. A switch that opened a floodgate of lust.

"My sweet wife," he said against her lips. "I will never get enough of you."

She fluttered her eyes closed and returned his deep kiss, their tongues dancing, their damp bodies meshed together.

His touch shifted, and he slipped past her hip, her upper thigh, and sought her cunny. He stroked over her needy spot that was already sensitive with want.

"Oh, Frank. No, we…"

"Do not deny that you want me to touch you." His voice was almost a growl as he circled her nub.

"Oh…oh…I am not denying that, but…"

"We are the lord and lady of this estate, and we will do whatever we desire."

"But what if someone sees?"

He pulled back and glanced around. "We are hidden by the reeds, do not fret."

"Are you sure?"

"Yes." He slipped his caress further between her legs and probed one long finger into her cunny. A slick cool ride that felt so good.

She moaned and let her head fall back. He caught her crown in his palm and ducked to kiss her neck. Soft little brushes of his lips and tongue that sent shivers over her flesh.

She gripped his thick shoulders. Her nipples were hard pebbles against his chest. Raising her right leg so her knee hugged his hip, she urged him deeper, wanting more and unable to control the urgent craving inside of her body.

"Dear Lord, you drive me wild," he said hotly against her ear, then nipped her lobe. "So damn beautiful."

"Frank…oh…I…"

"Find your pleasure, now, here." He rubbed over her sweet spot, giving her what she needed.

She screwed her eyes up tight, the pressure building almost instantly.

"I want to watch you," he murmured, slipping another finger inside her and pushing deep.

She gasped at the delicious stretching.

"You're exquisite like this, *mon ange*."

She canted her hips forward and back, riding his hand in the water, his thumb fretting her nub as his fingers lodged deep. It was all she could think of, reaching that pinnacle of bliss with him holding her like this.

"Good Lord, yes," he said, keeping her in a tight embrace. "Like that. Just like that."

She tensed, her teeth gritted and her heart thudded so hard her pulse drowned out all other sounds. Even the water felt hot now, as if she'd caused it to boil around them.

"Take what you need," he said hoarsely. "Take it."

She did, a swift hard climax that had her biting on her lip to stop from crying out. It flashed over her body like a bolt of lightning—spreading ecstasy.

He hovered his lips over hers as she panted through the bliss. "Sweet, beautiful, Anna."

"Oh my…oh…yes…oh, Frank…"

"I've got you," he said, still working her.

She rolled her hips, taking the last of her pleasure. "It's so…oh…it's so…"

"Good in the water?"

She moaned and dropped her head forward into the crook of his neck. Her cunny spasmed around his fingers, and she was aware of a warm gush of release.

He found her mouth and kissed her, filling her with his taste. She became aware of the sound and feel of his breathing. He was aroused, too. Enjoying himself.

"Frank," she managed. "What about you?"

"Me?"

"You…you're hard."

"That I am. But I will wait until nightfall for my release. This was all about you."

"I don't understand."

"I wanted your first experience in the water to be memorable. It will bode well for learning to swim."

She giggled. "I'm sure that is quite an unconventional teaching method, Viscount De-Wold."

"You should know by now." He slipped his fingers from her and pulled his hand from the water. He cradled her face, drips running down his arm and off his elbow. "I am not a particularly conventional fellow."

"Yes, that is something I do know about you."

He kissed her again and then, "Come, lets enjoy our picnic, we have worked up quite the appetite."

CHAPTER SIXTEEN

Four weeks later…

T HE DOWAGER HAD been confined to her bedchamber for weeks, and Anna felt beside herself with worry over the situation.

Frank had said to give it time, but how long did that mean? Was he to let her die in there of old age? Spend the rest of her days alone?

The guilt was beginning to gnaw at Anna like bedbugs that wouldn't leave her be.

"I trust you slept well?" Mary busied herself with the heavy curtains, fussing so they hung neatly in their swags.

"Yes, very." Anna glanced at the pillow to her right. It still held the dent from Frank's head. "The viscount left early for the factory?"

"He did, my lady. Just after sunrise, so I heard."

"He's excited about the new arrival of stock from India. So am I, in truth. It is apparently of exceptional quality. Perhaps I will get some new frocks out of it."

"That would indeed be very nice." Mary lifted a tray of food from the table to the bedside. "Would you like me to pour your tea, my lady?"

"Yes, please." Anna smiled and sat higher, her shoulders resting on the softly feathered pillows. She watched as Mary poured the tea from the pot to the cup, the little brown stream tinkling as it hit the china. She added a splash of milk.

Anna's stomach turned over.

"Here." Mary smiled and passed it over. "Would you like a slice of pound cake? It's freshly baked this morning."

Anna held the tea, the sickly smell of the milk catching in the back of her throat.

She swallowed. "Er, no, thank you."

Mary appeared surprised. "Are you sure?"

She swallowed again and closed her eyes, rested her head back.

"Oh, my lady, are you unwell?"

"I certainly don't feel well this morn, although I was perfectly fine yesterday."

"Was it something you ate at dinner that has disagreed with you?"

"No, I don't think so. If I recall, it was artichoke soup and then mackerel. Quite tasty. His lordship commented on how fresh the fish was."

"Yes, we had a delivery from Hunstanton yesterday. How the cart had held onto all that ice in this heat I don't know, but it was packed full."

Anna bit on her bottom lip and handed the cup and saucer to Mary. "Please take this. Perhaps I'll drink it in a moment or two."

"Of course." Mary quickly set it aside.

Anna's stomach tightened as if a fist was gripping it. She blew a breath out through pursed lips and hoped the prickling sensation peppering her forehead would soon pass.

Mary squeezed her hand. "Should I fetch a doctor, my lady?"

"No, no." She shook her head. "I'm just feeling a little queasy, that is all." She paused. "Though I'm not usually inclined to nausea."

"You are making me quite worried about you."

"It will pass. But thank you."

For a moment they sat in silence, then, "My lady, can I ask you a question?"

"Of course, Mary, you are my dearest friend here, if you cannot ask me a question, I don't know who can." Anna managed a small smile.

"And you are very dear to me." She hesitated. "But I cannot help noticing you haven't had a moon bleed since you arrived at the De-Wold estate."

"Moon bleed?"

"Yes, a monthly bleed," Mary spoke in a lowered tone. "It comes around with the full moon, or for me at least it does."

"Oh, I see what you mean." Anna was suddenly a little flustered. "I guess...no, you're right, I haven't. Although I am fortunate, and it is not usually very bothersome."

"Then you are lucky." Mary smiled. "And if that is the case, I might be wrong about what I am thinking."

"Whatever are you thinking?" The sweat popping on her brow was receding, and the fist around her insides had eased. The threat of imminent vomiting had faded. Thank goodness.

"I'm sure you remember from what your mother, your aunt, cousins told you." Mary tipped her head. "About the way of nature."

Anna wracked her brain. Mary was talking in riddles, which was so unlike her. "I had no aunt or cousins and what my mother told me...I'm not sure what you are referring to?"

"About being in a certain situation."

"Certain situation?" Anna shook her head. "Please Mary, I really don't know what you're talking about."

Mary cleared her throat. "You have been married for two months, am I correct?"

Anna thought for a moment. "You are."

"Please forgive me for asking, but was the marriage consummated at the beginning?"

"Oh well I..." Anna's cheeks heated. "Isn't every marriage?"

Mary smiled and nodded a little. "I'd like to think so. Because when a marriage is consummated, it means..."

"What? What does it mean?"

"It means that you can become with child."

"Oh my!" Anna slapped her hand over her mouth. "You think I am with child? So soon? We have only just married, and..."

"A single night time union of a husband and wife is all it takes, or so I am led to believe."

"Oh, my goodness." Anna couldn't possibly count how many times she and Frank had laid together, found pleasure together, clung to each other in ecstasy late at night—during the day when the opportunity arose. Why just the previous evening he'd flipped her onto her stomach and given them both extreme pleasure by candlelight.

"Are you not pleased, my lady?"

"I don't know what to think." She shook her head. "With child." Placing a hand over the blanket covering her lower belly, she closed her eyes. It was impossible to deny that she hadn't hoped to carry Frank's child one day. Produce an heir for his title, estate, and business. But this quickly...that is what had taken her by surprise.

"My lady, you really do appear quite shocked."

"I am. I mean...I remember my mother telling me I was born just nine months after she and my father married, but I hadn't thought much more of it."

"Good fertility is often passed down from mother to daughter."

"You are very knowledgeable on these matters."

Mary giggled a little. "I have three sisters all older than me, two are married. I also have four female cousins who like to talk about all manner of things when we get together and we are away from gentlemen's ears."

"Oh, I see." Anna couldn't imagine having so many women in her life to discuss such things with.

"I may be wrong," Mary said. "I am no midwife or doctor."

"No." Anna pulled in a deep breath, her chest puffing up, nipples tingling oddly. "I believe you. It is the only explanation."

Mary grinned suddenly, and her eyes flashed with what looked like excitement. "A new baby in the house will be wonderful. And I promise I will do everything I can to help you."

Anna reached for Mary's hand this time and gave it a squeeze. "I know you will, and that makes me feel braver about this entire situation."

"I am sure you will cope admirably with both pregnancy and childbirth. You are young and strong and of a determined nature."

"I hope you are right."

"And his lordship will be very pleased. When will you tell him?"

"Soon, I don't think I could possibly keep my suspicions from him. He would know there was something on my mind immediately."

Mary nodded as if in agreement. "Can I get you something? Iced water a ginger biscuit perhaps."

"Yes, both of those sound more agreeable than tea and cake. And if I feel better afterward, I will dress and go to the library and wait for the viscount. I enjoy the view of the lake from there, and there is a copy of Defoe's *Robinson Crusoe* that I have been eager to indulge in."

"Very good, my lady." Mary stood. "I will be back shortly with a breakfast that befits your condition, and after that I will help you dress."

"Thank you."

Mary left the room, and Anna closed her eyes. She listened to the sound of her breaths and felt her lungs expand and deflate. Was she breathing for two now? Yes, she was sure she was. A rush of anticipation rushed through her. Oh, how she longed to hold her baby, but at the same time there was such a journey ahead. And when she thought of Frank taking a tiny bundle into his arms, meeting his son or daughter for the first time, her eyes welled up with emotion. She wanted to make him happy and proud. She wanted to give him everything he deserved. Her husband was the most decent, kind, wonderful man to have ever walked on God's earth.

TWO HOURS LATER, Anna made her way to the library wearing a pale blue gown that hung straight and to her ankles. She liked its comfort and simplicity and the delicate white Huguenot lace that sat around the sleeves, neckline, and flounce.

The library was a grand room that she always enjoyed spending a few hours in. Unlike the library in the London townhouse, this was sectioned in two by a grand arch decorated with murals. The window was an enormous bay affair set with cushioned seating to give readers a place to sit with a breeze and a view.

She turned the corner, passed a vase of peonies, and went in through the heavy oak door.

A woman stood at a shelf. Her scarlet dress hung to her ankles, revealing ribbon-tied matching sandals and her dark hair was piled high in a series of pinned curls.

"Oh." Anna came to a halt. "Dowager, I did not expect to see you in here."

Bertha didn't look up from the open book. "I will not be long."

"No, please, take as long as you wish." For a moment, Anna wondered about turning around and leaving but then thought better of it. This was the first chance she'd had to speak to Frank's mother since their arrival and her blast of vitriol.

She let the door shut heavily behind her and walked to the shelf she hoped to find *Robinson Crusoe*. Once there, she ran her finger over the titles written in embossed scrawls on the spines.

The only sound in the room was the ticking of a clock on a high mantel. After a few minutes, she found the book and withdrew it. "I am so pleased to have found this book," she said. "I have heard good things about the story." She waited, hoping to have started a conversation.

But the dowager made no response.

"May I ask what you are reading?" Anna asked, turning to face Bertha. "You appear totally absorbed, perhaps I will move to that book next."

"You may have it now if you wish, as you are the new viscountess, or so it seems."

Anna's heart ached. Judging by her mother-in-law's words and tone, there had been no mellowing since her arrival. "I would not wish to take something from your hands if you are enjoying it."

Bertha turned. "Yet you have taken both my son and my home."

The ache turned to anger, but Anna quashed it down. "Your son is still very much your son, I can assure you of that. I wish for nothing more than for you to continue to love one another and spend happy times together."

Bertha's lips tightened.

"And as for your home," she smiled and gestured around, "it is plenty big enough for us all."

"Yet you are the new viscountess. Which means you must take up the duties of organizing staff and menus, decoration and finances."

"And you are doing these things at present?"

"Yes, and I have done so for many years, I find it quite easy even though it is not."

"Would you like to continue with all of those duties?"

"I find them...yes, I like to know what is on the menus, and it is important to have the right staff." She paused, tilted her chin, and

151

appeared to look down her nose at Anna. "I have made mistakes in the past."

"We all make mistakes. We all must grow and learn from them and ultimately be forgiven."

"If that is what you believe."

"It is." Anna walked toward the window seat clutching her book. But halfway there the room began to spin. The bookshelves became a blur. The floor slid left and right as if she were on the deck of a ship, undulating, wobbling, her knees weak.

She gasped and came to a halt, reaching blindly for something to hold onto. There was nothing but thin air. She swayed and staggered, black ants were crawling over her vision. "Oh, my goodness." She pressed the back of her hand to her brow, the sweat was popping again, and that fist had returned to grip her insides.

The next thing she knew, she was sliding downward. Her weak knees no longer able to hold her upright. Her spine was crumbling, her head too heavy for her neck.

"Viscountess! Anna!" Bertha's voice was strange and distant, as though coming from underwater. "Oh, my goodness! Help, someone help us. Quickly."

Anna wanted to open her eyes, speak, continue a conversation she hoped would lead to a resolution of their situation. But she could do nothing. Her eyelids were too heavy, the blackness too alluring.

She slipped toward it and let the dark envelope her like a thick heavy blanket. Warm and secure in its embrace, she drifted away, away from the dowager, the library, and even herself.

It was a blessed relief.

"Oh, my lady, please wake up."

Someone was speaking to her.

"My lady, please squeeze my hand. All will be well."

It was Mary's voice.

"Come back to us, that's it, open your eyes." A tap on her cheek.

Anna tried to do as Mary asked and squeezed her hand but failed to open her eyes, her eyelids were still too heavy. She let out a groan.

"She is coming round," Bertha said. "Isn't she?"

"I'm sure she will now her legs are raised."

Anna thought about what Mary had said, and yes, sure enough it felt as though her legs were up on a cushion of sorts.

"What on earth is the matter with her?" Bertha asked. "We must send for the doctor immediately. Get the smelling salts. Oh, I have some in my reticule on the table."

Anna tried to speak Mary's name. The word was on her tongue, but it wouldn't come out.

"Here," Bertha said. There was a swoosh of material at Anna's side. "Let's try this."

A sudden overpowering scent of vinegar and something bitter and noxious attacked Anna's nose and lungs.

She gasped and coughed, her eyes springing open as she tried to push herself forward and escape the ghastly smell.

"My lady, you are awake, thank the good Lord above." Mary pressed her palm to Anna's forehead.

"How do you feel?" Bertha's face appeared next to Mary's, her brow creased and her eyes wide.

"I...I...I'm not sure." And that was the truth. It had all happened so fast—yet Mary was in the room now, and she had not been a second ago.

"It's all right," Mary said. "You had a little fainting attack, that is all."

"Yes, it is rather warm in here." Bertha nodded, her attention still firmly on Anna. "But the window is open now, so air is coming in."

"I, er, thank you. Thank you both."

"Shh, don't try and speak, catch your breath. Is your head spinning?" Mary asked.

"A little." Anna pushed herself to sitting and locked her arms behind herself. A rush of light-headedness besieged her, but she breathed through it, glad to be seated even if it was on an oriental rug.

"What on earth is going on? I heard from a footman when I alighted the carriage that...oh my goodness, Anna." Frank rushed into the room, still wearing the tail jacket he'd worn to the office. He tossed his hat to one side. It rolled onto the floor. "Anna, what has happened?" He kneeled down at her side and clutched her hand. "My love."

Mary, who was jostled out of his way, quickly stood. "She came over all faint for a moment or two, my lord."

"That has never happened before." He looked at his mother. "What was said between you beforehand?"

"Nothing to cause a young woman to faint," Bertha said with indignation. "And as soon as I realized what was happening, I summoned help in the form of her lady's maid. And now I shall call a doctor."

"No, no, please, a doctor will not be necessary." Anna shook her head. "Please, can I sit on the couch?"

"Of course. I will help you." Frank slid his arm around her.

"And I will get you a glass of water," Mary said, standing. "As tea is not suiting you today."

"Tea is not suiting you?" Frank said.

"Please, just help me up, I feel like a fool on the floor."

"Of course."

His arms were strong and solid around her as he helped her to standing. For a moment, she paused, closed her eyes, and took a deep breath.

"She's going again," Bertha said. "Here. The salts."

"No, no, I'm not." Anna was determined to stay on her feet. "Please, just the couch." She opened her eyes again and saw Bertha rush to the couch and plump a cushion.

"I am worried about you," Frank said.

"Don't be, it's over now, I'm sure. I feel better already, especially now you're here."

"I will never let anything hurt you." He pressed a kissed to the side of her head, then gently helped her sit.

He sat close and took her hands in his, his big fingers wrapping around her small ones. "Is there anything I can get you?"

"No, Mary has gone for water."

He lifted her knuckles to his lips and kissed them. "What a fright you gave me. I cannot bear the thought of anything happening to you, my one true love."

"Oh, Frank." She looked into his eyes. "I'm sorry. I did not mean to give you a fright."

"Do not be sorry, just be well. For without you, I would never know happiness again. My life would be colorless." He paused. "You are my reason for breathing each day."

"I feel the same." She reached for his cheek and stroked her thumb over the place his dimple appeared when he grinned. "It has only ever been you, and it will only ever be you."

"My lady." Mary was at her side, holding a tray with a glass on it. "Your water."

"Thank you." Anna took a sip. It was cool and refreshing and instantly made her feel better. She smiled.

"Color has returned to your cheeks," Mary said, "which is good. A lady in your condition shouldn't—" She clasped her hand over her mouth. "Oh!"

"In what condition?" Frank asked.

"I'm so sorry," Mary said, her lips down turning. "I didn't mean to…"

Anna's heart rate picked up, and she quickly took another sip of water.

"Sorry for what?" Bertha studied Mary and then Anna. After a moment, her eyebrows raised. "I see!"

"What is going on?" Frank asked a little sharply.

"I…" Anna paused, she wasn't cross with Mary for giving up her secret, in fact, she was relieved because it couldn't be a secret. "I believe I am with child." She'd studied Frank's expression as she'd spoken. "We are going to have a baby."

His mouth fell open. His eyes widened. He closed his mouth and then a smile tickled the edges of his lips and they tilted, it turned into a grin, a full-on beam with dimple on show. "You are?"

"I'm as sure as I can be."

"My love." He cupped her face and glanced down at her belly. "You really think our child is conceived, is growing as we speak?"

"Yes. I do." It was as if they were the only people in the library such was the joy of their news. They were all that mattered, she, Frank, and their baby.

"My goodness me." Bertha sat with a bump on the couch at Anna's side. She wafted the salts beneath her own nose and breathed deeply. "This is turning out to be quite the morning. All most unexpected."

Frank released Anna and reached over her lap to take Bertha's hand. "Mother, it would please me very much if you could be happy for us. If you could accept this marriage and in the future the baby."

"Well." She closed her eyes in a long blink. "We are clearly well past any chance of an annulment." She gestured to Anna's belly. "If a child is on the way, hopefully a son and heir to continue the Webb name and the De-Wold estate, might I add." She paused. "And as for being happy for you, Frank. I believe I can be."

"You can?" Anna said. "You will be?"

Bertha nodded and almost smiled. "Yes, for I love my son, Anna, and if you bring color to his life and give him reason to breathe, how can I not be pleased to have you at his side?"

"That brings me great joy to hear." Anna felt as though a weight was being lifted from her shoulders. Like gravity had suddenly halved and she could run and dance and float if she wanted to.

"Besides," Bertha went on, "Defoe's *Robinson Crusoe* is simply one of the best novels I have read, so you clearly have excellent taste in literature, my dear. We have that in common at least."

Anna held in a giggle but not the huge smile. "Thank you, Dowager."

"Do not thank me, for we have much to make up for." She slid her salts away and stood.

"We do?" Frank said.

"Yes." She raised her arms. "We must throw a party, a grand party, a celebration of your marriage."

"Mother, I really think—"

"How many people attended your wedding? Your breakfast?"

"Er, just the two witnesses and then for our wedding breakfast, there was only us in attendance."

"Only the two of you." Once again, the dowager raised her arms. "That is preposterous, you are a viscount, your marriage should be a lavish affair."

Frank laughed and stood.

Anna got the feeling he, too, felt like a weight had been lifted.

"Mother, you do not have to go to all the trouble of a party." He reached for her hands. "Really you don't. To have you pleased for us is enough."

"Nonsense, a party is exactly what we need to shake away all of this glumness." She laughed. "And what is more, we shall hold it next week, before my daughter-in-law begins to show, because that would take the fun out of choosing a new gown, wouldn't it." She looked at Anna.

"I, er, yes, I suppose." The thought of a grand party scared Anna a little, but she knew she would have to get used to being viscountess and throwing such parties herself one day. It was the way of her new world.

"Of course I am right." Bertha released Frank's hands and turned to Mary. "I need you to go and tell Cook I will be down to the kitchens shortly to discuss the menu for the feast, and inform the footmen they will be taking out invitations this very afternoon. Also, we must get the ballroom painted, the walls are scuffed, and I must arrange for the florist to visit so we can plan the decorations. What floral preferences do you have, Anna?"

"I'm really not sure." She glanced at Frank, but he clearly didn't have an opinion on flowers. "I'm happy to go along with your suggestions, Bertha, your taste is always exquisite."

"Yes, it is." She half spun in a circle, then stepped up to the couch and swiped up her reticule. "I must go, there is much to do. Mary...why are you still standing there, go, go and do as I have instructed."

"Yes, my lady." Mary bobbed, then rushed from the room.

The dowager was close behind her.

"Well." Frank said putting his hands on his hips. "I only went to the mill for a few hours, and it seemed everything happened while I was gone."

"Yes, it has been rather exciting."

He sat at her side and pulled her into his arms.

She rested her head on his shoulder and closed her eyes. "Are you truly pleased about the baby?"

"How can you even ask that?" He stroked her hair. "I've been the happiest I have ever been these last few months with you as my wife, and now, to know we are to start a family, I feel like I have been truly blessed, God has given me everything and more. I am the luckiest chap on England's shores, that I truly know."

CHAPTER SEVENTEEN

"W HY, MY LADY, I have never seen you more radiant." Mary clasped her hands beneath her chin and sighed. "Pregnancy becomes you."

"Thank you, Mary. But I have you to thank for my hair. You have done a wonderful job."

"Your hair is easy to work with, my lady."

Anna smiled and turned her head to once again admire the chignon. It was utterly perfect, as were the small ringlets that framed her face. A delicate dab of rouge reddened her cheeks, and her lips were stained the color of the deepest red roses in the De-Wold formal garden.

"His lordship will adore your dress, I am sure."

"He has not seen it yet." She spun the other way, and the dress swished around her legs. Light and long, it was made up of several layers of white silk. The puffed sleeves were square and the material gathered just below the bust line. A vertical panel from hem to neckline was embroidered with hundreds of tiny golden flowers.

She smoothed her palm over her still-flat belly, pressing the soft material to her flesh.

"Would you like another ginger biscuit?" Mary asked, reaching for a blue and white china plate that held several.

"No, thank you. Two should suffice to hold off any nausea, for a while at least."

Knock. Knock.

Mary smiled. "It is time to say hello to your guests, my lady."

"Not many of whom I know."

"But you soon will, for you are the new Viscountess De-Wold."

"Yes, that is true. Wish me luck." Anna took a deep breath.

"You don't need it. They will all be utterly charmed by you." Mary opened the door, and Frank stepped in.

"Ah, *mon ange* you are ready and looking particularly delightful." He stepped up and took her hands in his, surveyed her from head to foot. "How are you feeling?"

"I'm well, thank you. I took to my bed for most of the afternoon."

"As you should in your condition." He pressed a kiss to her cheek. "Come, let's not keep our guests waiting."

"Are there many here yet?"

"A few and more by the minute." He paused. "Are you sure you're well enough for this?"

"Yes, it's just…I'm a little nervous. I'm not used to being the center of attention at a party."

"That is understandable, but just remember, I will be at your side not as a viscount but as your husband, and if you need to step away for air, all you have to do is say, and I will take you."

"Thank you." She smiled. "The last thing I want is another fainting attack for all to see."

"That won't happen. I won't let it, I promise."

"Here, my lady." Mary passed her reticule, which matched her dress perfectly. "Enjoy yourself. I'll have peppermint tea waiting for you later."

"You're a godsend, Mary. Thank you."

They went arm in arm down the grand staircase—which had been extravagantly decorated with peach and cream carnations. Frank going slowly and carefully, treating her as if she were a fragile ornament, which had been the case since she'd told him she was carrying his child. She'd never felt safer or more loved than she did at her husband's side.

"Sadly, my good friend the Duke of Hillcrest cannot make it," Frank said. "I'm disappointed, for I wished for you to meet him, but equally I am not surprised."

"Oh? Does he not like a party?"

"No, he really doesn't, in fact, he confessed once that it was his idea of hell."

"Those are strong words."

"I agree. But he is a loner, content to rattle around his enormous home and do little other than paint." He paused. "Or at least that is what he tells me."

"Frank." She looked at him. "It sounds to me as if you know more."

He chuckled. "Only that I know from our last conversation that he was hoping to find company, female company, and had a plan to find a wife, or at least that was the impression I got from him."

"That will be quite a task if he does not leave home."

"Mmm, I agree." He squeezed her hand. "All I can hope is that when I next see him, he has news."

The gentle sound of a string quartet drifted toward them, and when they reached the base of the stairs, they were quickly swept up in a tide of polite greetings.

There were so many people to make acquaintances with, Anna's cheeks soon ached with smiling.

"Ah my dear, you have arrived." Bertha floated over to them wearing a long peacock-blue gown, heavily beaded and with puffed sleeves. Her dark hair was draped in a thick curl over one shoulder and a peacock feather rose from her crown, pinned in place.

"Mother," Frank said with a smile. "You look radiant."

"Not nearly as radiant as your bride." She smiled at Anna. "Your hair looks simply stunning, my dear."

"Thank you." Anna bobbed her head politely.

"And the dress." Bertha's chest puffed up. "Madame Bouffant is incredibly gifted, and to have created this in a week, simply marvelous."

"I agree, it is no wonder she has been your dressmaker for so long. I am thrilled that you introduced me to her. I cannot see me using anyone else going forward."

Bertha's lips tipped into a satisfied smile, the way they always did when Anna acknowledged her wisdom over all things a viscountess should know. Sometimes she felt like she was in training, even though she was actually on the job already. But that suited her. If Bertha was happy, then life at the De-Wold estate was much easier for everyone. And besides, she would have her hands full when the baby arrived. It suited her to let Bertha keep hold of the reins...for now.

"We will have to order a christening gown at Christmas," Bertha said, "so we know we have it."

"Very wise, Mother." Frank took two glasses of champagne from a passing waiter. He handed one to Anna.

She took it with a smile, but knew she wouldn't drink more than a sip. Wine made her queasy these days, and she was sure the same would be said of champagne.

"The flowers are simply beautiful. Thank you for organizing them." Anna gestured at the high-ceilinged, pillared ballroom that was lavishly decorated with great urns, spilling over with peach and cream blooms of every kind. Thick glossy ivy dripped from each urn, almost reaching the floor.

"I find a simple color scheme works the best," Bertha said. "And doesn't distract from the architecture."

"What a good idea, I'll remember that."

"Ah, Lady Burghley." Bertha lit up at the sight of a woman about her age wearing a gown the shade of a bruised plum. A step behind her was a handsome couple arm in arm. "I am so pleased you could all make it."

Lady Burghley set an air kiss alongside each of Bertha's cheeks. "I wouldn't have missed it. And how charming you look, Dowager."

"And the same goes for you, Duchess."

Lady Burghley smiled and took a glass of champagne. "Congratulations to the happy couple." She nodded at Frank and Anna.

"Thank you." Frank dipped his head, as did Anna.

"I hear it was a whirlwind romance." Lady Burghley's eyes glistened as if hoping for gossip.

Anna felt Frank tense.

"Not in the slightest," the dowager said, tipping her chin. "My son and the new viscountess have known each other for many years." She nodded over Lady Burghley's shoulder. "I see your family also has marriage news."

"Ah, yes." Lady Burghley spun around. "May I introduce the Duke and Duchess of Farrington." She beamed. "The duke is my new son-in-law."

"Duke, I am pleased to make your acquaintance," Frank said. "Duchess, it's a pleasure to see you again."

"Oh, please call me Elizabeth, we have made acquaintance in the past."

Elizabeth.

Anna snatched in a breath as a memory came flooding back to her. Lady Elizabeth Burghley, of course, the young debutante Bertha had invited to visit Frank the day after she and her mother were expelled from the De-Wold estate.

The image of Elizabeth and Frank greeting each other had been like a kick in the gut, and the sight of them walking arm in arm toward the lake to get to know each other had been a stab to the heart.

She tightened her hold on Frank's arm and took the tiniest sip of champagne.

"Viscount, Viscountess, it's a pleasure to meet you both. And my wife and I would like to offer our sincere congratulations." The duke, whose accent held a Scottish lilt, smiled warmly. He was tall with olive skin, as though he spent a great deal of time outdoors, hunting and riding, no doubt, and his hair was thick and blond with a few streaks of amber running through it. In a blue tartan kilt and matching plaid, he had a regal air about him, broad shouldered, straight backed, confident. He wasn't entirely clean shaven, as all the other gentlemen at the party were; his trip to the barbers had obviously been a few days previous.

But that didn't seem to bother his wife, the Duchess of Farrington, who gazed up at her husband with adoring eyes. If Anna wasn't mistaken, her gown just skimmed a rise on her abdomen. Was she expecting, too? If so, she was keeping it a secret. The reason why...? That was none of Anna's business.

Anna cleared her throat. "Duke, Duchess, thank you for gracing us with your presence."

"We wouldn't have missed it," the duke said. "Though I am grateful we traveled here from Burghley and not from the Kilead estate, which would have been a far longer journey."

"Where is Kilead? If you don't mind me asking." Bertha raised her eyebrows.

"Not at all," Elizabeth said. "It's in the Scottish Highlands. Simply beautiful."

"I have heard good things," Frank said. "Apparently the hunting is exceptional."

"It is, you must come and visit, I will take you out onto the moors. But plan appropriately, there are some months it barely gets light, and other months the midges will eat you alive."

"That sounds…testing," Anna said.

"It can be." Elizabeth nodded and then smiled at Anna. "But I am learning that the majesty of the mountains makes up for the pitfalls. And besides, we always have Burghley to lodge at."

"Lodge at?" The duke raised his eyebrows at his wife.

"You can't deny, you like a lodge, husband."

They both laughed, it was clearly a joke between the two of them.

"And you have a second book in production I hear," Bertha said to the duke.

His eyebrows raised as though surprised she knew. "I have, thank you for taking an interest."

"Really?" Anna said. "How exciting. What is it about?"

"It is a wee collection of poetry." The duke pressed his hand on his chest. "Though while I am rather proud of it, I am even more in awe of my wife since she has just signed a deal with a publisher in Edinburgh. Her first book will be available next summer."

Elizabeth smiled, and a little rise of color bloomed on her cheeks. "You must enjoy the praise for yours, Tom. Next summer is a long time away."

"Aye, but my book is simply words, yours is art, too."

"And pray, can I ask what yours is about, Elizabeth?" Anna asked.

"Of course, it's a documentary of the flora of English woodlands. I'm hoping it will be an accurate reference for years to come."

"What a truly talented couple." Frank nodded. "Our hearty congratulations on your accomplishments."

"Thank you." The duke smiled. "That is most kind of you."

"I really must introduce you to Lady Clement," Bertha said to Lady Burghley. "Shall we?"

"Of course." Lady Burghley smiled at Frank and Anna. "Congratulations again."

"My dear, would you like some champagne or a claret?" the duke asked Elizabeth.

"A claret, please."

"Then come, let us find you some." The Duke of Farrington nodded at Frank. "Perhaps a smoke later?"

"I would enjoy that very much."

The pair walked into the throng of the crowd, admiring glances following them.

"They are a handsome couple," Anna said.

"Er, yes, I suppose," Frank agreed.

"She is very pretty."

"Is she?" His brow creased.

"As pretty now as she was back then."

"I beg your pardon?"

"The day after that…incident, she arrived, all elegantly titled and beautifully turned out and apparently ready to take my place in your affections."

"Oh Anna." He lowered his face to hers. "I barely heard a word she said to me during the entire visit. I was bereft at your leaving. My heart was breaking. I was simply going through the motions of being polite, and at the same time trying to figure out what I could do to get you back."

"Which you didn't."

"Er…I beg to differ." He lifted her hand and touched his lips to her ring. "Wife."

She giggled, won over instantly by him. "Yes, you have a point."

"And on which note." He glanced around. "I think it is time you took a little break from being sociable. I do not wish you to become tired from too much company."

"Really?"

"Yes." He began to steer her up the staircase. "Just a few minutes, alone, in the cool of my room. It will do you good."

The sight of his tense jaw and the flash in his eyes sent a scurry of anticipation wending through Anna. She knew that look only too well.

It was a delicious mix of determination, mischievousness, and eroticism.

"Frank?"

"Hurry, I do not wish for us to be interrupted."

"From what?"

He didn't reply, and when they reached the top of the stairs, he urged her past several family portraits and an occasional table she remembered seeing beside the schoolroom years ago—it still held the same vase.

When they reached his bedchamber door, he shoved it open.

"Are you quite well?" she asked as he ushered her through it.

"I will be." He closed the door and leaned back on it, blew out a breath.

"Whatever is going on?" She rested against him, hands on his chest and spoke onto his lips. "You seem all out of sorts."

"It's you." He wrapped his arms around her.

"Me?"

"Yes. You're so beautiful, and you're mine. I look at all the other women, wives, and it makes me realize again how lucky I am to have you, the kindest, most witty, well read, pretty...I could go on."

"I love that you think that."

"And I love you." He kissed her, deep and intense as if solidifying his words with his lips.

She felt her heart rate quicken, and her breasts pushed up against her clothing. A familiar heat spread between her legs.

"I keep thinking," he said, "about that day in the garden...when we..."

"Got caught doing something we really shouldn't have been doing."

"Yes." He peppered kisses over her cheek, and cupped her buttocks, pulled her closer. "That."

"Oh!" She caught her breath. Beneath his clothing his cock was steely hard and wedged against her. "I can see the memory has had quite an effect on you, Viscount."

"It has." He pressed his mouth to her ear. "Though now we are married, there is nothing indecent about you putting your hand down my breeches."

"I am sure some people would disagree."

"Ah, but would you?"

"No." She tipped her neck so he could kiss the sensitive spot behind her ear. A flutter of sensation went over her scalp with each touch of his lips. "I don't think...I would have a problem with it." Closing her eyes, she slid her hand between their bodies, to his breeches, popped open a couple of buttons, and slipped through the fall in the material.

He moaned softly.

This spurred her on, and she took his length in her hand. He was so hot and hard and thick.

"Stroke me," he said, his voice husky. "Do what you would have that day."

She tightened her fist around him and slid to his root and then up to his tip, swiping her thumb over his slit.

"Oh, in the name of the dear Lord above," he groaned, dropping his head back to the door and closing his eyes. "More, like that."

A wonderful rush of power went through her. She had her handsome, strong, sometimes wild husband completely under her control. Her love for him bloomed even when she didn't think she could love him more. Seeing him hand himself over like this, admit his fantasy, trust her to make it happen was adorable.

She worked him tip to base again, kissing the curve of his jawline and tasting a hint of perspiration.

He tensed and his arms around her tightened.

"I want you to spill your seed," she whispered. "Into my hand."

"I will...if you keep doing that."

"Good. Because I'm not stopping."

He moaned again, and she continued to work his hard cock. It twitched in her hand, and a slick of moisture leaked from the tip. "I love feeling you like this," she whispered by his ear. "My beloved husband."

"I'm yours," he gasped and canted his hips forward as though pushing into her fist. "And you're mine...forever."

"Forever and a day." She increased her speed and nipped his earlobe. "I am yours for eternity."

He grunted and then held his breath.

Excitement gripped her. He was close, so close.

And then it was there, he moaned low and guttural, almost animal-like as a pulsing wave of release bloated his cock. Warmth coated her hand, and she used it as lubrication as she stayed with him, jerking his length as pleasure gripped him.

"Ah...yeah..." he moaned. "Oh, Anna...that's it."

"Did I fulfill the fantasy?"

"And more." He caught her face in his hands. He was breathing hard. "Every day with you fulfills my wildest fantasies." He kissed her. A wonderful deep, breathless kiss that made her melt against him. His heart beat against hers, and she'd never felt closer to him or more loved and adored by him.

And the icing on her cake was that soon their first child would be born. A son with God's grace, the next Viscount De-Wold. She wanted to make her husband proud and happy every day for the rest of their lives.

She'd fulfilled his fantasy, and she was glad he'd dared to dream. Because for so long, when life was hard and uncertain and she was bound in grief and heartbreak, she hadn't known if there was a way out—she had not dared to dream. She'd hardly been able to think of Frank and what they could have had. The different path they could have taken.

But fate had intervened and brought them together in the most unconventional of ways. Her good fortune had come about thanks to nothing more than a late-night hand of cards.

Or had it?

Had the Black Widow planned her anonymous marriage to her first sweet love? Had she known that Anna and Frank belonged together? That only they could make the other happy?

Anna supposed she'd never know. She supposed she didn't need to know.

The End

Want more? Of course you do…

If you're wondering how Lady Elizabeth Burghley snagged herself a hunk in a kilt and a title to boot grab a copy of A SCANDALOUS SEDUCTION and get whisked off your feet in a heady romance full of passionate and forbidden interludes.

And don't miss the reclusive Duke of Hillcrest's kinky story in THE DUKE'S PET and find out if his very particular needs can ever be met.

Printed in Great Britain
by Amazon